T0156564

CARDINAL RULE

CARDINAL RULE

W. GREG HENLEY

CARDINAL RULE

iUniverse books may be ordered through booksellers or by contacting:

iUniverse
1663 Liberty Drive
Bloomington, IN 47403
www.iuniverse.com
1-800-Authors (1-800-288-4677)

Because of the dynamic nature of the Internet, any web addresses or
links contained in this book may have changed since publication and
may no longer be valid. The views expressed in this work are solely those
of the author and do not necessarily reflect the views of the publisher,
and the publisher hereby disclaims any responsibility for them.

Any people depicted in stock imagery provided by Thinkstock are
models, and such images are being used for illustrative purposes only.
Certain stock imagery © Thinkstock.

ISBN: 978-1-4917-8494-5 (sc)
ISBN: 978-1-4917-8495-2 (e)

Library of Congress Control Number: 2015920920

Print information available on the last page.

iUniverse rev. date: 01/19/2016

For Tyler

We have grasped the mystery of the atom
and rejected the Sermon on the Mount ...

—General Omar Bradley

... whatsoever ye would that men should
do unto you, even so do ye also unto them:
for this is the law and the prophets ...

... Ye have heard ... Thou shalt not kill; and whosoever
shall kill shall be in danger of judgment ... but I
say unto you that every one who is angry with his
brother shall be in danger of the judgment ...

—Jesus of Nazareth
from the Sermon on the Mount
Matthew 7:12 and 5:21–22 ASV

CHAPTER 1

A Good Landing

For an instant, the massive energy generators came to life and, in a single burst, channeled their combined energy into the starship's mass dampers. And for just that instant, the starship's inertial mass fell to nearly zero, the rocket engines were ignited, and the starship executed its plunge down to sub–light speed. In the viewfinders lay the blue-green world of Galton III (although at that time it was still known by the letters and numbers of the standard classification system), unchanged from the images sent back to Earth from the old robot ship *Lewis and Clark*. The robot had made its brief flyby visit to this Earth-type planet a full half century earlier. But so many such planets were being found that it had taken a long time to assign a manned survey ship to this unremarkable world. This mission of the USS *Cutty Sark* was routine. No celebrations and no steak dinners with all the trimmings were awaiting this crew's return to Earth. They expected nothing but a continuation of the boredom of deep space as they set about their tasks of interpreting new sensor data while their captain ordered the ship into a standard polar orbit.

The polar orbit would allow the efficient surveying of the planet's surface. The first manned interstellar missions had been made only after extensive robot reconnaissance—so that the manned expeditions had detailed maps and surveys on file when they arrived at their destinations. But as interstellar expeditions became routine, such preliminary surveys were now infrequently made and then were made as ancillary missions such as this mission of the *Cutty Sark*, especially when the destination appeared to be as ordinary as this one.

The ship's first lieutenant and chief navigator, Reginald G. Greene, peered intently at his three-dimensional display of the planet's system. In addition to the planet, the display showed one large moon and one very small one. A blue line recorded the ship's progress, and an extended red line forecasted its projected course. The red line, now a circle around the planet, was being traced by the blue line. Greene reported to the ship's captain, "Stable polar orbit, Captain. All scanners read clear. Communication reports no activity. Recorders are running. Radar and visual mapping under way."

"Very good, Reggie. Send home a probe with a current log. Have Engineering inspect the generators and mass dampers. And have a course plotted to the nearest outpost. I want to be able to get out of here in a hurry, if we have to. Have the department heads meet me in the mess hall in thirty minutes for debriefing. I want an update on what life signs we have. I want to know if there are any threats out there. I'll be in my cabin until the debriefing." The professional routine continued as Connors unlatched the heavy bulkhead door at the rear of the control room and made his way to his cabin. Connors appreciated Greene's efficiency. They had served together for a long time, and Greene had acquired the ability to anticipate his captain's requests. A preliminary survey of the planet was no doubt well under way, and the captain was fully confident it would be ready in time for the debriefing.

Connors stood leaning over the tiny sink of his cabin's small galley, eating a ham sandwich and reading his mail on his private monitor before going to the briefing. An unmanned courier probe had just delivered the mail. (Signals could, in those days, still not be transmitted at hyper-light speeds, so messages were sent by probe to prearranged locations for broadcast.) First he read the official dispatches. Then he checked his personal mail. There was nothing there except some letters from his family, two magazines that were not available in the ship's library, and a stack of typical junk mail—including a bunch of offers for high-adventure action and pornographic holo role-play movies. He could do without those. Some people would sell anything for credits. Connors believed in freedom of the press but wondered where responsibility entered into the equation. Then again, he knew pilots who ran contraband rather than working behind a desk—anything to keep flying. And he knew lawyers who represented clients in causes that they knew were unjust—just because they needed the credits. He figured human nature allowed them to somehow rationalize it away or just not think about what they were doing. After all, few sane people really saw themselves as the bad guy, no matter what they did. He deleted all the movie titles and closed the mail file. He would read the letters later.

Despite Greene's efficiency, Connors could never really relax from the time his ship entered a star system until it was safely in orbit. There were just too many things that could go wrong, and at the speeds they traveled, a lot of damage could be done real fast, despite the ship's repeller fields. Connors had heard what had happened to the USS

Villeneuve when it had slammed into a planetoid while entering the familiar space of Epsilon Eridani. The *Villeneuve* had an aggressive pilot who had, unnecessarily, entered the system too hot—that is, too fast—which unfortunately threw the ship slightly off its planned trajectory. And he had gone in through the ecliptic, which was a mistake in the first place. He had easily steered through the outer planets, but the closer he got to the inner planets, the more crowded space became and the busier steering and repelling became. He was steering *Villeneuve* through a very graceful S turn around two large planetoids when an asteroid, eclipsed by the second planetoid, came into view in the ship's path, with another asteroid to its starboard quarter. The pilot had begun swinging *Villeneuve* to port when another planetoid suddenly loomed in the center of the ship's forward view screen. Before there was time to react, *Villeneuve* had cleaved the planetoid in two, and all that was left of the ship was the hulk of the reinforced crew module. Fortunately there were other ships in the area. The crew was saved but not the career of *Villeneuve*'s captain. Connors did not want to see either his ship or his career come to the same end. And so he seldom relaxed. This was his ship and his crew. He knew that their actions were his responsibility, and he constantly reminded them that "for every action, there is an equal and opposite reaction, whether intended or not"— such was the philosophy of a spacehound.

The department heads were in the mess hall gathered around one of its six four-meter-long, firmly anchored tables. They were reviewing the latest photo images when Connors entered the room. They stopped and turned to face him.

Smith, the senior scientist and head of the Exoanthropology Department, greeted him with the service's typical understatement. "It looks like we've found something interesting, Captain. We've found some definite signs of an advanced technology but only limited signs of current habitation. As a preliminary estimate based on plant growth, we figure there was a depopulation between seventy-five and one hundred fifty years ago. We'll need more information to make a better estimate. We don't know enough about the biology or the causes to be more precise. The causal event or events could have happened overnight or over a long period of time. We really can't tell right now."

"I don't like surprises."

"We missed it with the long-range scans," explained Greene. "We didn't eyeball it, and the computers weren't calibrated for it. But when we got closer, we started a Phase III search. We looked closely for signs of primitive development in the vicinity of natural harbors, river junctions, and the larger mountain passes—the usual places. At first we still didn't see anything. But that was just because the planet is so overgrown with vegetation. Basically the cities are so gone to weed that it's as if they're camouflaged. But there are cities there, all right. Probably at least equal to late-twentieth-century technology. Smith gives it a seven to eight on the Craig scale. Some of the ruins are over fifty stories high."

"Any radiation?"

"Nothing significant."

"How about signs of climatic changes?"

"It's hard to tell, but probably not," Smith answered this time. "And the change would've had to have been very sudden. Otherwise a technology apparently this advanced could have adapted."

"What about cratering?"

"Apparently not, but we're still reviewing the new maps."

They sat looking at the photomaps. Climate maps showed the planet to be mainly temperate. Radiation maps did show some isolated hot spots but not enough to kill a planet. On the whole it seemed a lot like Earth, except its atmosphere was slightly richer in oxygen and it had a weaker magnetic field. But little could be determined about its biology.

The theories about what had happened to the planet started to get numerous and wild. Someone hypothesized that the entire intelligent population had either left or been taken away. Someone else guessed that the botanical life *was* the intelligent life.

It was finally agreed that what was needed was more information, particularly soil and air samples. Unfortunately, the *Cutty* had no robot ships capable of a two-way trip to the planet's surface. One of its two robots had been left behind as a scientific station at the mission's very first target—a planet that had proven to be very similar geologically and biologically to cretaceous Earth. The second of the robots was lost to a malfunction when it was blasted with a geyser of molten uranium while hovering over a volcano on one of the moons of Sutter V. Now, with no robots, the *Cutty* would have to limit itself to orbital surveys and only report the planet worthy of follow-up. But such an interesting planet seemed too good to leave to another ship.

No one was happy with the turn of events that had left them without a suitable robot. Twenty-twenty hindsight told Connors that he should have been more miserly with his robot deployment, but there had been no reason to expect either the loss of the second robot or the uniqueness of the current find. And he knew it would be bad for the crew's confidence, discipline, and morale if he acted like he doubted his past decision. If the planet had turned out to be no different than what the *Lewis and Clark* had reported, there would be no need for a landing. They could just make some maps and head back to base. And Earth would not consider the mission a failure if they still did just that. After all, this was their third planet-fall, a secondary target to their main mission of making geological maps of Sutter. They could get enough basic information from orbit so that the next ship could come with a specialized crew and training. But what Connors really wanted to do was go down there.

It was Greene who broke the impasse. "I think I can take a small team down in a lander," he suggested. "I'll limit my crew to a first officer, a flight engineer, and a four-part survey crew—a chemist, exobiologist, exoarchaeologist, and exoanthropologist. We'll use containment suits and follow complete Level IV protocol, including decontamination in the airlock before and after each trip outside. We'll get some quick samples, take a fast look around, and come straight back."

Connors had to agree. He had wanted to make the suggestion himself but did not want to put anyone in the position of feeling like they had to volunteer. He knew his place was with the *Cutty Sark*. As usual, he could count on Greene. He told himself that he did not like the idea of part of his crew being exposed to such a high degree of potential trouble while he, the captain, was safe in the ship. But he knew that in reality he was just jealous; this would be an interesting ground mission. And he also knew that Greene was the designated lander command pilot. The mission was rightfully Greene's. He agreed to the suggestion and subtly let Greene take control of the mission's planning. Greene punched up a map of the planet and asked the specialists for suggestions for a landing site.

Connors glanced out the mess hall's view screen at the world that seemed to glide beneath the ship. He knew it was inappropriate for him to stay and manage the details of the ground mission. It would be bad for Greene's own authority and training. With hidden envy, he told Greene to give him a complete report on the mission profile within the hour, and he left the mess hall.

Cutty Sark's maneuvering engines glowed white hot as the two-hundred-meter-long vessel swung laboriously around to an equatorial orbit to prepare for the mission. It was early morning ship time, and it would also be actual early morning in the landing zone. This coordinated the landing party's biological clocks with landing zone time and would provide maximum daylight. All ninety-one of the remaining crew watched from view screens as the lander detached from the *Cutty Sark*'s outer hull and began to maneuver slowly away and behind the starship. To Connors, the arrowhead-shaped lander looked especially graceful in space. The alien sun glinted off its clean white surface as it turned to fire its main engines for the descent. Connors always felt a bit romantic about landings. Gravity dampers used too much power to be useful to landers. So landers still used chemical engines not that different from those of the early days, when the first astronauts rode modified ICBMs into the edge of space. That was space travel. Running the *Cutty Sark* was more like managing a business.

But the memory of the *Villeneuve* brought Connors back to reality. He looked to his left. There sat the ship's chief engineer, his panels connected by telemetry to the lander's instruments so that he could monitor its systems and progress. Greene reported that all was "Go." The engineer concurred. Connors gave the final "go" sign, and the automatic landing sequence was switched to *enable*. The engineer confirmed the computer's countdown to zero—an unaccountably ancient ritual. Then the lander's main engines fired into life.

In the atmosphere of Earth, the roar would have been deafening. But in the vacuum of space, there was nothing to be heard. A variation of the old riddle, "If a tree falls in the forest, and there is no one to hear it, is there sound?" Maybe no sound carried to the *Cutty Sark*, but there was no question that there were tremendous energies at work here.

"We're programming in rotation A-OK," Greene reported as the engines cut and the lander turned and rolled to direct its belly nose-first toward the onrushing atmosphere.

As the lander slid out of orbit, final checks were made of its flight systems. Contact was lost as it fell below the horizon, but the orbits were coordinated such that the *Cutty Sark* was making an overflight of the landing zone during the lander's planned touchdown, so that communications could be reestablished and maintained during the landing. Everything was ready for the final descent.

Long moments passed as the delta-winged vehicle shot through the planet's upper stratosphere in the hottest portion of entry—when the hull temperature would reach 2,800 degrees Fahrenheit and the G-forces would be their highest. Then, having survived the atmospheric braking, the ship's skin began to cool, and its hotspots no longer glowed red. Still traveling at supersonic speeds, its double sonic boom rumbled beneath it across the planet's surface.

A white contrail marked its progress across the blue alien sky. It was in this terminal phase of the flight that something went terribly wrong.

"*Cutty Sark*, we've got some kind of a malfunction here," Reggie reported.

Connors turned to his chief engineer.

"Captain, they just lost about every system. I've got red lights all over the board."

The next voice was Jake's—the lander's flight engineer. "I don't know what's going on, *Cutty*. I can't pinpoint anything that would cause all these simultaneous failures. But the situation has stabilized."

"I've got her under control, Captain." That was Reggie again.

Then there was static.

The chief engineer turned to face Connors. "Captain, I'm getting no telemetry."

Connors turned to his assistant navigator, who was tracking the lander with his navigational instruments.

"I've got their current trajectory, Captain, but I'm picking up some strong interference. I'm afraid I'm going to lose them. The trajectory is not ballistic—they must still be under some control."

Greene was glad he had a real windscreen to look through and not just an electronic reproduction. Otherwise, he figured, he'd be flying blind. As it was, he was having enough trouble just seeing down past the lander's up-tilted nose at the planet's surface. He checked himself. He realized he had better start thinking in terms of "ground" real fast because it was starting to get very close. His arms were aching from the strain of piloting with the backup, hydraulic controls. Even those pumps were dead. But he figured impact was just a long minute away. He began a broad S turn. He was bleeding off altitude and aiming for a lake that looked like the best place to set down.

"You better get back up here, Jake," he called over his shoulder, just as his flight engineer appeared from behind and strapped himself in.

"No luck, Reggie. I can't get a darn thing to work. No radio, no engines, nuthin'. I even climbed down into the engine bay. The circuit breakers are home, the power's there, but the actuators won't engage the igniter circuits.

"Sorry. Just give us one we can walk away from."

"Very funny."

Greene was glad he had spent a lot of time in sims. Although he had never simulated a complete systems failure, because they were not suppose to be possible, he had simulated a few dead stick landings because he always took everything one step further than by the book. But a dead stick *landing*, if he could call it that, into water was a new one. He slowly came out of his turn and lined up on final approach. He let the nose up a bit. The lander was no boat, but he figured if he did this just right he could use the water to cushion their impact and then let momentum carry them up onto the beach. Besides, there was no choice. It was either the lake or plow through a whole forest of trees. He stole a glance at Eric, who was trying to help with the strain on the stick. The manual stick was a throwback to the old days, and he was lucky to have it. But then again, the pilots had all banded together and demanded the hydraulic stick and pedals—those and the windscreen they could really see out of. Eric sure looked unworried. He was probably confident that Reggie could land the thing. One somehow always had confidence in his shipmates' abilities to do their jobs; it was only ability that got them where they were. But that did not stop Greene from wondering if they were going to wind up as a new crater some 150 light-years from home. As they came in over the trees at the near end of the lake, Greene realized that at least he was calm. He was thinking clearly. There was no panic. He was passing the test. He was just doing his job. The training and practice had worked. But he failed to give himself credit for the quick yet calm and focused thinking that had gotten him into the service in the first place.

He could feel Eric helping him strain against the hydraulics. Now they were over the broad lake, its small waves rippling silver in the sun. Down there it was calm and peaceful—a complete contrast to the descending mass of straining flesh and spacecraft. The ship was nevertheless steady and quiet as it glided over the tranquil waves. The only disturbance was the light whisper of air over the spacecraft's wings.

The tranquility was abruptly disturbed as the lander hit the water and sent up cascades of crashing and surging water. Reggie and Eric pulled full back on the controls and fought to keep the nose up and the wings level—fighting with the ship against burrowing under, flipping, or cartwheeling. They surged along for what seemed an eternity, yet the beach and trees ahead of them loomed quickly closer. Soon the trees filled the windscreen—an impenetrable green wall. Then suddenly, they jerked to a stop.

Greene could see through the windscreen that the lander had come to rest at the edge of the beach, with its nose just ten meters up on the bank. Two-thirds of the lander was in the water, but it seemed to be basically level and sitting solid. He wasted no time.

"You okay, Jake? Eric?"

They each answered a confidant "Okay."

"Okay, then I want you two to suit up and go outside to look for propellant leaks. And try to determine how secure we are. I'm going to go back and check out the engine bay and the others." It was then that what must have been the last functioning control circuit clicked into operation. It was a warning indicator, the steady high-pitched chirp of an audible signal accompanied by the flashing red warning light indicating a hull breach.

Aboard the *Cutty Sark*, the navigator was straining to sort clues out of the interference blanketing his sensor data. The chief engineer was tuning his instruments, trying to reacquire the lander's telemetry. The communications officer was scanning the lander's five preset transponder frequencies. Suddenly, all interference with the instruments stopped. But there was still no communication or telemetry from the lander.

Connors requested a plot of the lander's possible landing and impact locations. The navigator and engineer based their resulting calculations on the lander's flight characteristics, last known conditions, and trajectory. They presented the captain with a triangular plot of the lander's possible impact and landing points, with the lander's last known location as the apex.

The apex represented a hypothetical nonaerodynamic impact point. If the vehicle had simply broken up and fallen with no aerodynamic control, it would have impacted at the apex. Fanning out from there was the broader section of the triangle representing an unpowered dead-stick landing. And from the altitude they were at when the troubles started, they could have gotten pretty far. Their possible track stretched out a full one thousand miles. At the center just inside the base of the triangle was the planned landing site. The base was an arbitrary limit. In reality, a powered lander could have landed anywhere on the planet. But an assumption was made that the lander's crew would try to stay close to the planned landing track, whether the lander was powered or not. Connors ordered a full sensor search, with the plotted area to be the first area searched.

Connors knew that the search would be a long process. There had been no response from the transponder, telemetry, or voice communications. The area to be searched covered over 160,000 square miles. Magnetic resonance and other sensor sweeps were already proving ineffective due to the indigenous artifacts and the lander's shielding. The most useful results were expected to come from the optical scanners. And even though the scanners could pick out objects as small as the latches on the lander's doors, the problem was knowing exactly where to look. The computers would help by searching for shape patterns similar to the lander's, but crash damage, obstructions, and misidentifications always complicated computer searches. It was going to be an exhausting search. And there were still no ideas as to what had gone wrong.

Aboard the lander, things were settling down. Jake and Eric confirmed that the lander was sitting stable. The hull breach had caused no immediate problems. And no one in the landing party was injured. But almost every electrical circuit was disrupted.

Paul, the chemist, had extended the lander's atmospheric probe and collected a sample of the planet's air. He was doing his best to perform an atmospheric chemical analysis within the limited capabilities of his damaged personal survival kit. Elizabeth, the exobiologist, was conducting a similar analysis of the atmosphere's biology. But without their computers and electronic testing equipment, they accomplished little. They were on a dead planet and could not determine what agent had killed it. And with the hull breach, they had all been potentially exposed to it. Even if they could return to the *Cutty Sark*, they would have to spend weeks or months in the isolation of quarantine while the researchers made certain that no disease was taken aboard. Greene was determined as anyone that the *Cutty Sark* not become a plague ship. But he did not relish quarantine, which would be his fate unless they found the cause of the planet's problems. Until they knew it was not biological, they would have to assume that it was. And the only way to do that was to identify it. Until then, the unknown was just too great a risk. Greene knew that many viruses could lay dormant for years before manifesting themselves. Therefore the causal agent or event would have to be identified and dealt if it could endanger the crew.

Reggie gave the two scientists a few hours to get organized and begin their research and then had everyone meet in the lander's small galley to compare notes. Jake had hot-wired the lighting system so that they had light. He had also gotten one of the environmental system's blowers going and was circulating the lander's air through the chemical scrubbers. At least that would keep the air moving and the humidity down, which would make them less uncomfortable. And with the external temperature at 33 1/3 degrees Celsius (ninety-two degrees Fahrenheit), the inside temperature was beginning to climb, so anything to make the internal environment more agreeable was appreciated. Reggie asked each officer to report.

Because the immediate problem was their being able to live in the planet's environment, he started with Elizabeth.

"The air's chemistry is breathable," Elizabeth began. "We were able to establish that before we landed. To determine if there are hostile biological agents, I've started cultures and completed some basic tests, but I'm not going to be able to do much unless we get the rest of our equipment working."

Jake reported next. He knew the lander's systems better than anybody. Getting it operational would be up to him. But he did not have good news.

"We have battery power, but I've yet to figure out what happened to us. The computers and control circuits are all dead. But I tested compression, and the hull breach was minor. If nothing else, we can wear pressure suits into orbit. From what I can tell, there is really no serious structural damage. Once we solve the electrical problem, I can have her space-worthy in half a day.

"The hard thing to explain is the failure of our personal equipment, because their logic, memory, and power circuits are separate from the lander's. But this could still indicate a computer problem. Even our personal equipment interfaces with the lander's central computer. So it could have been a computer glitch, either hardware or software. It's possible that the computer signaled for power boosts throughout the whole system, causing each subsystem to overload and shut down. But it would have had to bypass the safety overrides to do it. That doesn't really seem very likely, and it doesn't really explain why they don't reboot. But right now it's the best guess I've got. It's possible that the subsystems aren't rebooting because they're waiting for a reinitialization command from the central computer that just isn't coming. I'm going to rig a power line straight from the batteries directly into the computer's inlet power feed. I'll see if it does any good to bypass all of the intermediate controls and power trunks. If that doesn't work, I'll bypass the central computer to see if I can get some life in any of the subsystems. That would help isolate the problem. But I'm pretty much at a dead end. When I tried to get the environmental system going, I had to hot-wire a blower just to get air moving. If I had a new flight computer, I could patch together and reroute what we need to make orbit. Unfortunately, the *Cutty* doesn't have any spares—just subunit modules. Besides, we have to establish what caused the failure or it might happen again."

"Okay. Jake, keep it up. Getting the computer going would solve a couple of our problems." Reggie turned to Eric. "How are communications coming?"

"Nothing yet. The ship's transmitter and receiver are both dead, just like everything else. So are the ones in the survival kits. The transponder isn't working either."

"I'd like to at least let the *Cutty* know where we are."

"Jake and I have an idea on that. We can hot-wire one of the landing lights so that we can use it as a signal light. It'll sure mark our position clearly enough. And if anybody here knows the old Morse code, we can communicate."

"Good work. We'll figure out some kind of code. Try to have the light ready tonight.

"Here's our plan. Elizabeth and Paul will try to determine what chemical and biological threats we're up against and what threats we present to the planet. Eric, I want you and Jake to rig that signal light. While you're doing that, I'm going to take Judy and Mark to have a look around."

Aboard the *Cutty Sark*, Connors was holding a meeting of his department heads.

"Not only do we not have any answers, we don't even have any clues. You've all had six hours to get me some. I need each of you to tell me something new. I don't care if you think it directly relates to our problem or not."

The chief scientist began to sum up what each of the departments had to report. "Well, Captain, we have uncovered some evidence of electric generation on the planet. Some is hydroelectric, some is coal-powered, and some is geothermal." He pressed a handheld button, and a map of the planet appeared on a screen at the end of the table.

"As you can see by these electromagnetic traces, the planet has a total of fifteen measurable power plants. They're randomly spread out over the planet—at least there doesn't seem to be any pattern. We didn't find them earlier because we weren't looking for them. Frankly we had no reason to, based on the data from the *Lewis and Clark*. When we passed over this area," his pointer circled a mountainous area the size of Texas," we faintly detected some stray atomic particles that could be from a nuclear power plant. We can't be sure because of all of the iron and magnetite in the mountains that dominate the local geology. We know that there's natural shielding there because we can see it in some of the outcroppings. A plume of hot water that we spotted in one of the rivers could be related to a cooling system, but it was untraceable once it disappeared under one of those mountains. There's a lot of geothermal activity in the area, so it could be totally natural. We're looking for related surface structures now, but the same problems are hampering our subsurface search.

"We've had no luck in finding the lander," he continued, "for the same reasons. There's too much interference from that same geology plus what we're getting from all the machine artifacts.

"Another unusual thing we've we found was a large but short burst of very fast atomic particles accelerated in the 500 MeV range that appeared at about the same time that the lander had its problems. It only lasted for a few seconds, and whatever it was, it's gone. It does not appear to have been a natural phenomenon."

"Any ideas?"

"Not at this time, Captain. But a lot of power would be needed to generate and accelerate that amount of protons to such high velocities. And as you can see from the map, the lander was just in the line of sight with that possible nuclear station when it had its difficulties. And although we can't localize where that burst came from, it very easily could have come from that general area. There may be a connection."

"What about the radar and radio interference?"

"We haven't been able to pinpoint that source either. It seemed to shift around. The transmitter could have been moving, but the signal source moved so fast that that's unlikely. It's possibly a multiple transmitter array rigged with alternate switching. Either way, it would seem it's been purposely hidden."

CHAPTER 2

Making Camp

Greene swung the outer door open and stepped onto the right-side forward area of the lander's delta-shaped wing. Judy and Mark followed and stood beside him. All three wore green containment suits with clear bucket-shaped helmets. Each suit was equipped with a system of air filters. The main object was to protect the alien environment from the earthlings, but the suits would also protect the astronauts. The uncomfortably hot and sweaty suits were to be worn whenever outside the lander. Despite the hull breach, Greene had decided to take all possible precautions short of using their completely sealed space suits. He wanted to limit exposure as much as practical.

Seventeen meters ahead up a steep embankment lay a dense deciduous forest. The brilliant white sun hung midway in the blue alien sky. The air was thick with the moisture and breath of the forest. Greene latched the escape ladder to the wing and made the short climb down to the narrow expanse of coarse vegetation that separated a narrow beach and the nose of the lander from the edge of the woods. Mark, the exoanthropologist, and Judy, the exoarchaeologist, climbed down beside him.

"Let's see what we can find." Reggie's voice was low and muffled but audible through the thin plastic of his helmet.

Mark suggested following the vegetation along the edge of the beach to look for game trails. "A game trail would give us a good path into the woods and would probably lead to feeding grounds, sheltered areas, and even other watering holes. Any of those would also attract intelligent life-forms. And game trails are frequently used by ILFs as convenient natural roadways. But for that reason I do advise caution."

They headed along the beach, hoping to spot a stream or other break along the edge of the forest. These were the most likely places to find one of the game trails they were looking for. After just half an hour's hike, they rounded a point, and the lander was blocked from their view. Before them they found a small natural bay formed by the mouth of a small river. At that point, Greene ordered additional caution.

"That's a natural location for an encampment or settlement. If there's intelligent life here, I don't want to just walk up to its front door. Let's circle around through the woods and come up on that river from the flank."

They climbed through the center of that point of heavily wooded, sharply rising ground as quietly as nonwoodsmen could walk; they made a lot of noise. But when the ten-minute detour was complete, they came up to the river some one hundred meters inland. Here, just beyond the top of the ridge of the small valley that had been carved out by the river, they could rest. Stepping closer to the ridge, Greene could, with his field glasses, look down to the river and see the line of a trail that traced the grass at the river's edge. The river itself was barely more than fifteen meters wide. Although its depth was indeterminate, it looked cool and inviting. But the three astronauts concealed themselves in the brush and watched and waited for signs of animal life. They did see some small rodent-like animals foraging among the rocks of a dried-up creek that ran down to join the river, a creek that evidently poured down from the ridge they were on only in times of heavy rain, but they saw no other signs of animal life except small birds. After waiting and watching for a full hour, Greene ventured down alone to investigate the trail. The others stood lookout, ready to signal him with a pebble thrown in his path if anything approached. Greene never stepped onto the path but chose his steps carefully to get as close to the trail as possible without leaving his own shoe prints. It was then that he saw the first signs of existing intelligent life—humanoid shoe prints.

The alien bipedal tracks were in dry mud in a bare spot on the trail. They appeared to have been made by soft-soled shoes, almost like slippers. That the tracks were in dry mud told him they were not fresh. As Reggie explored the nearby area, he found signs of an old campsite, including the dark and cold circular scar of a campfire. Judging from some debris that had accumulated on top of the remains of the campfire, it had been unused for some time. Yet it had no signs of having been rained on, so it probably was not too old. He could see what looked like small animal bones that had been discarded in the fire and guessed that someone had been hunting and cooking. Continuing to explore, he looked down to see what signs his own footsteps were making and decided that he could risk getting closer to the riverbank. Moving down closer to the water, he found marks at the river's edge that he guessed had been made by a small, narrow boat being pulled ashore. He walked along the bank toward the river's mouth all the way to the lake and was relieved that the lander could not be seen from there. Then he then made his way back to Judy and Mark, who were anxiously waiting to learn what he had found.

The two specialists wanted to research the campsite, but Reggie decided it was best that they stay away. He preferred to leave as few clues of their presence as possible that close to the lander. Instead, the three of them returned to the lander the way they had come. But they did take a detour. As they approached the landing site, they circled far inland to look for more signs of life.

The lake sat in a broad depression. A level forested area in front of the lander stretched three kilometers wide and one and a half kilometers deep before meeting the rounded foothills of an ancient mountain chain. The bank rose fifty feet from the narrow beach at an almost forty-five-degree angle such that the lander was not visible from the forest. The astronauts passed the lander well inland, cut down to the lake, and then returned along the shoreline to the lander.

As the three astronauts completed their first exploration, the sun was just touching the horizon. Silver-edged wavelets danced across the broad lake and gently kissed the shore. From west to east, the blue alien sky was turning to shades of violet and black with the setting sun. Occasional islands of voluminous, white cumulus clouds, darkened underneath in shadow, were painted silver edged where their tops caught the last of the light. In the distance, the Earthmen could see the stark white lander settled incongruously on the wild shore.

Approaching the lander, the crescent shape of one of the alien moons soon appeared in the darkening sky. Now they could see the glare of cabin lights shining through the cockpit windows of the flight deck. Jake and Eric were bringing the ship back to life.

From beside the lander, a broad beam of white light suddenly stabbed up and through the humid air toward the sky and then just as suddenly went dark. At its source stood Jake bent over a contraption that consisted mostly of one of the lander's landing lights. He held a wrench in both hands and was tightening connections between the end of a power cable and the light. Eric was at that moment making his way from the lander's battery compartment in the engineering bay after making similar connections to the cable at that end.

From the battery compartment, the cable led up to and along an access tube and then through an open maintenance hatch in the midpoint of the lander's fuselage just above the wing. From there it stretched across the top of the wing and then dropped down and snaked ten meters across the ground to a switch Jake had cannibalized from the engine compartment. From there it stretched the final three meters to the powerful beacon. Jake had rigged the switch that far from the beacon so that its operator would not be blinded by it.

After decontamination, the landing party gathered around the galley table and gulped down hot coffee and sandwiches that Paul had made (Jake had made a priority of getting the galley working because, he said, "high-octane" black coffee was necessary to keep his "valves from knocking" when he was "cranking out the high RPM necessary to get real work done"), while Greene devised a code for the beacon. It was now completely dark, and it was time to start signaling.

Greene admitted to himself that he was more than just a little apprehensive about shining a beacon up into the night sky when there were signs of unidentified intelligent life-forms being nearby. Nevertheless, they all sat around a campfire Elizabeth had built, while Reggie began sending up their signal—fifteen flashes followed by a pause, followed by eleven flashes, followed by a long pause, and then repeating. Reggie planned to have his crew take turns and continue this for four hours, which he knew would be plenty of time for the orbiting starship to receive their "okay" signal.

Overhead, the *Cutty Sark* was passing through the terminator into the planet's dark side. Every scanner was manned as the crew continued the search for their missing crewmates. But it was a computer that first detected the anomaly of the beacon and brought it to an operator's attention. Manual optical scanners were immediately targeted on that location. The flashing light of the beacon was plainly visible. And with image enhancement, it was even possible to see the lander and crew. Because of the unusual pattern to the flashes, Connors immediately suspected it contained a message and put the cryptographers to work on breaking the code. The message was easily translated to mean "okay." To signal back, a powerful work lamp was rigged as a beacon in the *Cutty Sark*'s cargo hold. These lights were normally used to illuminate large work areas when orbiting reflective mirrors were not feasible. The ship was then rolled onto its side, the doors to the cargo bay were swung open, and the answering beacon played across the heavens its own "okay."

The lander's crew knew they had been found.

As the early morning sun bathed the lander in its soft light, Captain Connors studied the latest scanner images and contemplated his next move. The photos plainly showed the landing party as they worked around the landing site.

After three orbits and continued work by the landing party, Connors saw that they had spelled out a message on the beach with logs, stones, and wet sand:

All elctrncs out.
Nd Env. Sc. Comp.
Wpns.
Mps.

Connors called another meeting of his chief scientists.

"I'm going to have to get some equipment down to the lander. What happens if I send down another one?" Connors knew the general answer but was pushing his scientists for specifics.

"Possibly the same thing, Captain." It was Smith, the chief scientist, who replied. "We've been working on a theory. It looks to us like the lander was hit with a manufactured particle beam. Such a beam could have fried the lander's electronics, but the crew would have been protected by the crew module's heavy construction."

"Is it a weapon or do you think it was some kind of accident?"

"Probably a weapon. We can't think of any other reason why those particles that we detected would have been manufactured and released like that. It certainly wasn't natural, and there is no other logical explanation for why such a beam would be generated and shot up into the air like that. It wouldn't be the by-product of any research or benign equipment that any of us can think of."

"Is the *Cutty* safe?"

"Probably, but we can't be sure how strong that beam can be cranked up. We could always engage our cruising screens. But we'd have to project them toward the planet, and that would wreak all kinds of havoc down there. I don't suggest it."

"Can you pinpoint the source?"

"That's the problem, Captain. It's a beam weapon, so the effects are pretty much localized. That makes it hard to pick up, unless you're the one being shot at. The particles are detectable because they tend to fan out in the atmosphere, but they're hard to pinpoint. It would require at least three to four tracking events to do it."

"We're going to have to take out that beam, so we'll have to know where the projector is. Begin by concentrating your search in the area of that nuclear power generating station we spotted, and include optical scans. Be ready at 0600 tomorrow. I need to get some equipment down to the landing party. I'll see if I can give you a few shots from that beam to trace at the same time."

He turned to an intercom, depressed the "Bridge" switch, and spoke to the officer of the watch.

"Get Chief Engineer Walters. Have him meet us here in the mess hall."

Connors turned again to his chief scientist. "So you think our screens would protect us?"

"Yes, sir. The particles we encounter at hyper light speed are much more lethal than what this beam generator seems to be projecting."

"Okay, then. What about the screens in the lifeboats— they're built to withstand extreme conditions?"

"They should be sufficiently screened for this. Yet a lifeboat and its screens are small enough that they shouldn't damage the planet. But I want to remind you that we are not certain how powerful that beam projector really is."

At that moment, the chief engineer arrived. The captain gestured for him to sit in the nearest chair.

"Mr. Walters, I want you to rig a lifeboat for an automated landing. Fill it with anything you can think of that the landing party might need down there. Use the message they sent us as a general outline. Talk to the department heads and see what they suggest. And be sure to send what they need to treat themselves for radiation poisoning. I want to be able to drop it at 0600 local time tomorrow."

After helping with the message, Reggie, Mark, and Judy headed along the beach "south" of the ship beyond where they had walked while returning to the camp the previous day, looking for more signs of humanoid life. They did find a game trail that skirted the edge of the lake but found no more humanoid footprints. Continuing their explorations, they followed a dry streambed up from the lake, climbed an embankment, and discovered what appeared to be the remains of a wide, black-colored, stone-hard unnatural pathway that ran alongside the stream but up out of the flood plain. It was heavily overgrown with plant life yet looked to be passable by foot. It appeared to be constructed of a gravel material bonded together by a tar-like product. The exoarchaeologist identified it as asphalt, a road-building material characteristic of petroleum-based technologies often used to support small but heavy land vehicles. The path went on to the lake edge from the forest at their left. Proceeding upstream, it ran along the dry streambed's narrow flood plain with a steadily rising hillside to its right. Downstream it turned left just before reaching the lake and ran along the lakeshore just above the apparent high watermark. The astronauts decided to follow the road into the forest. Because the road could be used as a footpath, despite the plant overgrowth, they decided to take precautions against meeting its other possible users. They climbed to the top of the heavily forested hillside and from there followed the course of the road. They moved slowly and made as little noise as possible as they weaved through the underbrush and across the dried leaves of the forest floor. With all their practice, they were getting quieter.

After just a ten-minute walk, they could make out some kind of mound next to the road, which did not seem to fit the geology. Assuming it to be unnatural, Reggie led them down to investigate. The mound proved to be the remains of a brick and wooden building that had fallen in on itself and was overgrown with vegetation. After obtaining some samples, they climbed back up the hillside and continued to follow the roadway. Shortly thereafter, they passed a single chimney, standing upright and alone, surrounded only by the charred remains of a burned-down building of indeterminable history. The explorers took some samples and moved on. Not long after that, they came upon another unnatural mound of rubble. It had an adjacent yard of well-made but weatherworn stone monuments, which Judy believed was a pre-event cemetery. She advised Reggie that the building was probably a religious facility of some kind.

When they rounded the next hillside, they came upon a nearly complete building. It was in a very narrow and short stretch of valley and so was better protected from the elements. On closer inspection, it also seemed to be better built—of steel and concrete rather than wood. It was surrounded by asphalt and contained two large bays, each half as wide as the roadway. It had large gaping openings where huge sheets of brittle silicate-based glass had served as windows, as could be told by the jagged teeth of the remaining broken pieces. The building appeared to have been a vehicle-fueling or repair station of some kind, which the exoarchaeologist confirmed was historically consistent.

The building had been completely stripped of useful items. The doors, furniture, light fixtures, even the wiring and plumbing were gone. But a treasure had been left behind. There, clearly visible inside its broken frame and shattered glass cover, hung what they knew had to be a road map.

While Green looked over their shoulders, Judy and Mark carefully sketched a copy of the map. It was too decayed to try to take down and bring with them. And although sections of it had decayed beyond legibility, Greene could still make out the outlines of the lake, the river they had discovered the day before, and the road they were now on. He made a mental note of markings that evidently indicated cities. Unfortunately, the map did not show elevations. But Greene could see that the road they were on went quite a distance before reaching a town. The road curved a great deal, and he guessed that this meant that it was following terrain so difficult that building a straight path was not practical, so it was following the natural path of the little river valley. Mountains, he guessed.

He could see on the map that the river they had encountered the previous day was formed by the joining of two smaller streams approximately eleven kilometers upstream from the lake. Two roads also met there. Greene noted the position of this junction against the relative position of the lander.

As soon as they were finished with the map, the astronauts headed back toward the lander the way they had come. They arrived at camp just at dusk.

As the sky turned from violet to black, a flashing light appeared moving across the sky among the first stars. It gave Greene a strange feeling. He knew that the light came from the *Cutty Sark*. He contemplated the culmination of learning, technology, and power that it represented. Just yesterday it was his whole world. Now it was unreachable. He watched the pulses of light. It was a pattern, a message. Six pulses, pause, one pulse, pause, thirteen pulses, and a long pause. Then it repeated. "Fam." What could that mean?

CHAPTER 3

Help from Above

It did not take long for Greene to figure out that the first six flashes of the signal meant "six," in this case, not "f." And so it was that, shortly after dawn, the landing party gathered outside the lander and searched the sky for signs of whatever it was that was supposed to happen at "six a.m." because their code system had no zeros.

The *Cutty Sark*'s stubby lifeboat plummeted from orbit without grace. It had detached from the *Cutty Sark* on the planet's far side so that any tracking systems that it later encountered would be less able to establish its point of origin. Then it had made three low orbits before beginning its final descent. The entry into the planet's atmosphere was made well ahead of what the lander's flight path had been. A lifeboat contains prodigious fuel reserves and all of those reserves were to be used in this landing. The plan was to attract the particle beam's fire but to evade being hit and thereby force enough shots that the origin of fire could be plotted. The beam did manage to take three shots at it, but the little lifeboat drilled in through the atmosphere under them. It was not following a ballistic flight path but instead zigged and zagged as it dived low and then used its remaining fuel reserves to sustain its altitude at less than seventy meters until it reached the lander's crash site. As it started its final descent, it had just enough fuel left for a soft landing. When it was just five kilometers up-range of the lander, it began releasing a plume of orange smoke to increase its visibility. The landing party could not miss seeing it, as it shot just fifty meters above their heads before disappearing over the trees. They could hear the roar of its landing rockets as it momentarily hovered over a clearing that was to be its landing zone. The astronauts ran up the embankment toward the sound of the rockets and the orange trail of signal smoke as the lifeboat touched down. Suddenly the sound of the rockets stopped. Greene ran forward through the woods, the occasional bramble tearing at his containment suit, and burst into a clearing.

The lifeboat had set down as programmed in the middle of a small grassy meadow. The golden grass, thin and tall, had been stirred into waves by the exhaust of the landing rockets. Covered with dew, the tall grass glistened in the morning sun. Interspersed among the grass were occasional tall, thin, green plants topped with delicate blue flowers, which appeared to rise and fall on the crests of waves like a fleet of miniature blue-canvassed sailing ships on a golden sea. The waves were just beginning to calm as Greene burst into the clearing. He hurried across the field to the lifeboat. Out of breath, he rested for a moment, leaning against the lifeboat's still warm side, where the others soon joined him. Several small fires had been started by the lifeboat's rocket exhaust. Greene opened the boat's main hatch, reached inside, and retrieved two canisters of fire suppressant. He passed one to Jake and the other to Eric and set them to fighting the nearest fires. He grabbed a third himself and joined the battle. He was surprised to see that the fires were quickly spreading and surrounding the lifeboat. As the blue flowers burned, they sent off flying globules of flaming sap that spread the fire. And although the containment suits were fireproof, they were not insulated, and the heat burned through to the skin, making it impossible to get close enough to use the suppressant effectively. The fire was out of control. Reggie called Jake and Eric back, and they all ducked into the lifeboat. Reggie, the last one in, pulled the hatch closed behind. Throwing the doors open to the survival suit locker, Reggie yelled to the others to help him and Eric struggle to get out of the containment suits and into the cumbersome survival suits. It was a time-consuming struggle to change into the suits, but it was time well spent. The self-contained survival suits were made for very hostile environments. They could withstand temperatures hotter than molten lead, cold as absolute zero, withstand micrometeoroid impacts, and shield the wearer from radiation, among other things. So they could easily serve as firefighting protection.

The fires had joined into one large conflagration surrounding the lifeboat by the time he and Eric had changed suits. Reggie had the others stay sealed up in the lifeboat for protection while he and Eric attacked the fire with the last canisters of suppressant. First they walked side by side and opened a corridor to the fire's outer edge. Then they split up and walked all the way around the fire, applying the suppressant. They reversed direction when they met on the opposite side and thus worked their way in toward the center. The suppressant extinguished the fire where applied and combined with the surface so as to block oxidation and suppress the fire's recurrence. It was soon extinguished.

Greene returned to the lifeboat, switching on the suit's external speaker as he walked. Judy swung the door open from the inside as he approached.

"Well, if that smoke doesn't draw us some attention, I don't know what will," Greene called out.

Eric stepped up beside him as the others filed out of the lifeboat.

"Eric, let's get out of these suits and then see what works in this thing. Jake, take inventory of what they sent us, starting with weapons. I want the rest of you to keep your eyes open for visitors."

Shortly thereafter, Greene slid into the lifeboat's left-hand command pilot's seat while Eric slid into the right-hand seat. They started a main systems checklist.

"Batteries?" Greene asked.

"Point nine five," Eric answered.

"Fuel?"

"Point zero five."

"Environmental systems?"

"Green."

"Communications?"

"Green."

"Ignition circuits?"

"On automatic, switching to manual, and off."

"Attitude control thrusters?"

"Switching to manual, and off."

"Autopilot?"

"On, indicates green, switching to off."

"Computers?"

"All show green."

"Shields?"

"Show green, on standby, switching to off."

"Gyros—one, two, and three?"

"All to off."

"Other primary systems?"

"Green."

"Secondary systems?"

"Green. All systems are green."

"Check. Good. Let's try raising the *Cutty*." Greene reached over and flipped a toggle switch marked "Ship to Ship" and spoke into a microphone he pulled up from the panel.

"Hello, *Cutty Sark*, this is Lieutenant Greene. Do you read me? Over."

The communicator had been preset to burst transmit at a frequency clear of jamming. It was Connors who answered. "Where have you gold bricks been? I know you like the beach, Reggie, but this is ridiculous."

"Sorry, Captain. We just got a little bit carried away, I guess."

"What kind of shape is the lander in?"

"All of the electronics are out. We're still not sure exactly what happened. We saw some sort of flash of light just as everything failed, but we don't know what it was. We have a hull breach, but Jake thinks he can make it space-worthy enough to make orbit."

"Reggie, we think you were hit by a particle beam weapon of some sort. Something definitely took some shots at the lifeboat, but we couldn't get a fix on it. And we've found evidence of a nuclear power station that was just on your horizon when your troubles started. Don't try to make orbit until it's sorted out. And treat yourselves for radiation poisoning—just to be safe."

"Understood, Captain."

"Did everything make it down okay?"

"Jake's taking inventory now. Did you get our shopping list?"

"You bet. We sent some stocking stuffers, too."

"Thanks, Santa."

"Reggie, I know you're in a bad position down there. But one way or another, we'll get you out. Is there anything else you want?"

"Yes, sir. I'd like some high-resolution photographs of the small stream or river that lies to the lander's left, relative north, from the place where that river meets the lake all the way up to and including the juncture with another stream about eleven kilometers east from the lake. I also want photographs of the road that runs along the lake relative south from the lander. Going east away from the lake along that road, there are some ruins that we investigated yesterday. In one of them we found a map, and I'd like to be able to coordinate it to modern conditions."

"Good work. I'll get the photos transmitted over the lifeboat's com link for you. Be careful. I don't want you killed off by whatever it is down there. But I also don't want you to contaminate the planet."

"Right. To minimize exposure, we're following protocol despite our problems. No one goes outside without wearing a containment suit. One more thing. I'd also like some pictures of the immediate terrain surrounding the whole lake. It seems like a natural humanoid habitat, but all we've seen are signs of one hunter, and those were old tracks."

"Humanoid?"

"Apparently. Just some old footprints up along that river."

"Be careful. Those pictures are hard copied in the packet we sent you. We knew you'd need that much. Anything else?"

"No, sir. We're going to finish our environmental survey and get the lander patched back together. Just let us know what you find out about that particle beam."

"Don't worry. We'll get you out."

"Landing party out, Captain."

"*Cutty Sark* out."

Greene flipped the ship-to-ship toggle to standby so that incoming signals could be received and returned the microphone to the instrument panel. When he and Eric got outside, the rest of the landing party were busy adjusting their weapons belts while Jake was finishing the inventory by checking the contents of a canister marked "Photos." They had been given hard copies as well as data sticks.

Jake soon began his report of the inventory; they had been sent an environmental science kit, three general field computers, and an exoanthropology kit. To support their research, the other scientists had also been sent a complete new set of test gear. They had also received a toy-size aero droid for photoreconnaissance and for retrieving samples from survey teams. The weapons cache included standard-issue synaptic scramblers, stun guns, mortars, a laser rifle, and a rocket gun.

The exoanthropology kit would be useful if the landing party came into contact with an indigenous population. With it, the exoanthropologist could manufacture the disguises necessary to blend in. Its software package included a crypto and language analysis program to help decode and translate local languages.

With the environmental kit, they would be able to analyze the local air, soil, water, and biological samples for threats to the landing party. They would also be able to isolate earth-born threats to the local environment. Once a threat was discovered, it could be neutralized.

Greene designated one general field computer to Jake for the work on the lander. They gathered what they could from the lifeboat, closed and secured the hatch, and returned to the camp to test the new gear and continue their work.

Later that day, Greene sat at the table in the lander's galley and studied the photographs of the terrain surrounding the lake. He was still worried about being discovered by unfriendly locals, but the photographs showed no signs of habitation anywhere near the lake. He felt a cool breeze from an air duct. Jake was making progress. First he had gotten the lights going, then the galley, and now more environmental control. Eric had spent the day helping Jake. Elizabeth and Paul had started their environmental analysis. Judy and Mark were helping with the environmental study by collecting and cataloging samples. Reggie had assembled and tested the one-meter-long robot plane and had checked the weapons. Now, as the sun climbed toward its midday zenith, Greene considered their situation. He was more optimistic. Now they had weapons. And they had the computers and other tools they needed to deal with the alien environment.

At dawn of the fourth day, Greene left with Judy and Mark to return to the ruins where they had discovered the map. Due to its delicate condition, they had left it where it was. Although they had copied it as best they could, Reggie knew they had missed much detail and wanted to make copies with the new recording equipment. He also wanted to scan it into the cryptoanalysis banks so that a language analysis and decoding could commence.

They also went back to the cemetery. Because its monuments were carefully and expertly crafted, Judy guessed that they were pre-event. Elizabeth wanted samples from the bodies. Analysis of pre-event tissues could possibly help establish a baseline for the humanoids' biology, despite the samples' assumed poor condition due to their ages and circumstances. Any information would presumably be better than none. As an exoarchaeologist, Judy was well experienced in obtaining grave samplings. Using the new sonic imaging equipment and core samplers sent as part of her standard equipment, she was able to take tissue and bone samples from a wide range of subjects with little difficulty.

It was an uneventful trip. They arrived back at the lander just before noon, local time. Greene told everyone to have reports to discuss over a late lunch.

This was the first meal since landing where everyone was relaxed. Judy kidded Elizabeth that she was spending too much time alone with Paul. Elizabeth kidded Judy that she was just frustrated because she hadn't found any really good graves to rob. Everyone kidded Jake about his spending more time with the lander than he ever had with his girlfriend. And there was a lot of kidding about Paul's cooking. It should have amounted to little more than heating the prepackaged rations, but Paul had tried mixing together some creative combinations that failed the taste test.

Greene finally turned the conversation to their work. "Tell me something. Is it Paul's cooking or this planet that's gonna kill us?"

Paul turned somber. "I can tell you not to drink this lake water. Elizabeth and I finished our toxicology studies. This lake is so high in chemical toxins that not much of anything can live in it."

"All we've found in it are some microbes, some sort of algae, and a species of fish that can probably live in about anything," Elizabeth added. "But by normal standards, this is a dead lake. We don't think that its condition is natural."

"The toxins we're finding were definitely manufactured," Paul continued. "They're mostly petroleum-based but not naturally occurring."

"We haven't done much yet except study the immediate environment," Elizabeth continued. "The lake chemistry itself can't be natural. It just isn't compatible with the other chemistry and ecology we're finding. And the few biologicals that are in the lake are so heavily contaminated that if anything ate them, they'd at the least get very, very sick. You definitely would not want to swim in this lake, no less eat anything that came out of it. And you sure wouldn't want to drink from it. But the surrounding forest seems pretty similar to most carbon-based ecosystems, except for the scarcity of animal life. We figure there's so little local animal life because of the condition of the water; it's just not a good habitat."

Greene was pouring his second cup of coffee. "I guess that explains a lot. It explains why we haven't seen any fishermen here and why we haven't found game trails leading up to the lake. It explains why there are no villages here. It explains why there aren't more people here. Does it tell us what killed the planet?"

"Not directly," Elizabeth volunteered. "There's ample plant and animal life outside the lake area. You've seen some game trails and even signs of intelligent humanoids. We think the lake is either one symptom or just an anomaly. Judy had the *Cutty*'s exoarchaeologists study some of their reconnaissance photos while you were away, and they spotted what they believed to be ruins of numerous chemical manufacturing plants and storage facilities around the lake and the immediate water shed. We're guessing that as the abandoned facilities deteriorated, they spilled their toxic contents into the rivers and the lake. This scenario assumes that the facilities were abandoned for some reason and explains what would happen afterward if they were. Certainly chemical plants would have been dismantled and decontaminated if they were found to be killing the ecology while the culture was intact. We think it more likely that the facilities were nonexpertly abandoned as a result of some sudden causal event and that it was not the event itself."

"I had photos transmitted down to me," Judy added. "I agree that the facilities were abandoned, not dismantled. There were pictures of storage tanks that definitely burst from the inside out. And it seems to be ongoing, as if some things are still breaking down."

"I guess it could still be a question of which came first, the chicken or the egg," Greene added. "I think we better go have a look. Judy, hand me one of those maps we copied from the ruins. Paul, here's the river we found on the first day. Are there any of these facilities you're talking about along here?"

"Yes, sir. One. Right here." He stabbed a finger at the map.

"That's about halfway to the river junction. Show me those pictures. That junction is a natural place for a settlement." He inserted one of the photos into the hard-copy input of one of the computers, and the photo image appeared on the monitor. He dialed a crosshair over the river junction and then punched the "zoom" and the "enhance" buttons several times each.

"There's a settlement there all right. And judging by these pictures, the inhabitants look pretty much like us. Mark, can you make us look like these people?"

"Sure, I could put some implants in your cheeks and forehead, some dye on your skin, and a little gene manipulation to lengthen your arms and reconfigure your ears. No problem. The costumes and equipment will be easier yet. At least you'll look like them from the outside." As part of his mission specialist training as an exoanthropologist, Mark had been taught how to use implants, other makeup, and gene manipulation to disguise a human to imitate other humanoid life-forms.

"Okay. I want you three," he indicated Judy, Mark, and Paul, "to go with me to that facility and the village. I want the four of us to be given alien disguises. I want Elizabeth to stay here to continue her research and to conduct a deep analysis of any samples we send back via the UAV." He turned to Mark. "When can the disguises be finished?"

"A week from today."

"Good, then that's when we'll leave."

During the following week, Mark manufactured and perfected the disguises. Growth-acceleration hormones and electrostimuli, the same technologies first used in the treatment of athletic injuries, helped speed the genetic manipulations.

At the end of the week, Reggie was able to look down and see that he had been given long, slender, blue-gray arms and long, slender fingers. Fortunately the hands of the aliens were much like human hands. Hand movement was often the hardest part to learn. Of course, getting used to a radically new physical appearance could be almost as difficult. It could cause reality detachment and alienation. This could have disastrous consequences during decision making. For that reason, only crew members with strong egos were approved for contact missions.

Reggie looked up and studied Mark's transformed hairless and ear-less head. Large membranes on the side of the skull served as eardrums. A nose situated in the center of the face was imperceptible except for two small centrally placed vertical slits. The eyes were large and slanted with small black pupils. The white of the eyes was crisscrossed with a web of purple lines. The extent of the alterations left little question as to why such manipulations sometimes caused personality changes.

The astronauts' blood had been shaded purple. That helped with eye color and skin tone and would help them remain disguised in the event of a minor accident. They could tell the blood color from close-ups of eyes in the photos. In all other respects, they were internally still human, except for the standard-issue language translators, which had been surgically placed in their skulls adjacent to their inner ears before leaving Earth, which they now activated. These microcomputers could monitor an incoming language, translate it, and then quietly repeat in English into the ear canal what had been monitored. Signals could sometimes get garbled, like a recording of a room full of people. But with practice, the translator could be very useful. They could even be switched on and off with subtle voice commands. To speak, Reggie would first have to say in English what he wanted to say, but in just a whisper to himself. His lips would not have to move and no one would have to hear him. But the voice pickup located just under the skin of the roof of his mouth would hear the whisper and transmit it to the translator. The transmitter would repeat the alien language translation into his ear. He would then in his normal speaking voice repeat the translation. Voice print identification filters helped prevent translator feedback. To help explain their faltering speech, the astronauts would claim to be explorers and traders from a distant village. Experienced users found that they needed only to think what they wanted to say, and the words just came to them. But more of the language code would have to be broken and downloaded into the translators before they could work effectively. Tests showed that the translators still worked. Reggie attributed it to the overengineering and multilayered redundancies built into all such bio-implants, as well as to the extra shielding of the crew module.

The earthlings knew little at that point about the alien verbal and body language. Basically they knew nothing about how the aliens communicated. So they were not ready for contact. But Greene wanted to be as prepared as possible. All was ready for the final step before first contact. It was time for close surveillance. Surveillance so close that inadvertent contact and its associated dangers were more than a mere possibility.

CHAPTER 4

A Chemical Plant

It was nearly dawn. To the east, a faint hint of gray was evidence of the approaching day. To the west, the sky remained black and dotted with stars. The exoanthropologist, exoarchaeologist, chemist, and command pilot stood next to the lander, making final preparations before leaving for the village. They checked their equipment and packed the materials they would later use to fashion clothing to add to their disguises. The clothing was mostly complete, but they needed to add finishing details. They still wore their containment suits, which they had altered slightly to fit their new bodies. It was the twelfth day.

The air was cool and clear as the four astronauts started their march away from the lander and toward the river. It would be a full day's march up the river to the ruins of the chemical facility. Reggie planned to investigate the facility and then make camp for the night. From there it would be another half day's march to the village. Reggie planned to investigate the facility and then make camp.

Without incident, they reached the same spot on the hill overlooking the river that they had reached on the first day. Then they headed back into the woods and dead-reckoned their way upstream parallel to the river but just out of its view. Occasionally they would move in close to look, sit, and wait and watch for signs of animal life.

It was late afternoon by the time they reached the ruins of the chemical plant. They could see it nestled alongside the river in the valley they were following.

They fought their way down the hillside through the brambles and other heavy undergrowth and made their way to what they determined to be the plant's administration building. This was a single four-story redbrick building. Gaping holes testified to where windows and doors had been. Going inside, they found the offices to be completely gutted except for fragments of mostly wooden furniture. Even the plumbing was gone. From there, they moved on to a large, windowless building that they could tell had been the plant itself. Anything that could be stripped out had been. Even the cracking towers were partly dismantled. Tests indicated that the facility had processed highly toxic chemicals. Toxic residues were in the processing systems and also stood in pools on the ground around leaking tanks that Reggie guessed had been too large to take away. Without the containment suits, the landing party's health would have been seriously compromised. Reggie wondered if whoever it was who had stripped the place knew the danger. But the landing party learned a lot. There were numerous signs and administrative bulletins on the walls, which they were able to upload to the mainframe's language banks. Soon they would be able to start translating.

They could see where the remains of a road worked its way diagonally from the plant up the side of the valley, to the left of the plant. At the top of the slope, they could see where a water tower had buckled at the knees and fallen part way down into the valley. Through a clearing made by it and the road, they could now see the ruins of more buildings. They had not seen them earlier because trees blocked their vision, and the site itself was so overgrown by trees that they were not seen in the surveillance photos. Reggie decided to investigate and led the party up the old road that, like the other, was now little more than an overgrown path.

As the astronauts reached the crest of the slope, they could see the partial remains of a wooden stockade surrounding the ruins of one of four large redbrick buildings. The stockade had been built of felled trees and, in places, concrete blocks. Some of the stockade had rotted and fallen in. Another part had burned.

Trees were beginning to grow in what had been a large parking and commons area in front of the complex of buildings. This area and just the one building were surrounded by the stockade. Judy and Mark studied the stockade walls while Paul obtained soil samples. Consistent with the buddy system, Reggie stayed close to Paul while he worked. Then the two of them went into the stockaded building.

Like the administration offices below, everything useful had been stripped away. But they could see from the remains of lab tables and sinks that this building had been a chemical laboratory. Judy and Mark soon joined them. Judy had made progress.

"Lieutenant, we can see that at least part of the stockade wall was battered down from the outside. We found the rotting remains of a battering ram, and it's obvious at close inspection that some of the stockade was broken in, not just rotted. And we think that the fire that we saw signs of was deliberately set from the outside. The burn pattern is consistent with that. Plus, we found the remains of burned torches at the periphery of that break in the wall as well as at a few others." She turned her head, glancing around the room they were standing in. Reggie interrupted her.

"I don't need an exoarchaeologist to tell me that this was used for habitation. I can see where stones were stacked as fireplaces next to the window. And those wooden frames must have been beds." He indicated a row of collapsed wood frames and rags he guessed had been bed frames and blankets.

"Yes, sir. I agree."

"Let's look around some more. I want to know more about what this building was originally used for. And I'd like to know what happened. Let's split into two groups and see what we can find. Meet back here in one hour. Paul, you're with me."

They found that each of the buildings was pretty much the same. But only the building inside the stockade had been turned into habitation. Some of its rooms had been used as individual apartments. Some held ten or more beds each. It looked as if as many as fifty people had at one time lived there. Paul guessed that it had originally been a research facility. This was based on the tables, cabinets for lab ware, and the large number of sinks found in the rooms. Holes in the floors marked where gas lines might have once led to burners.

When the landing party got back together at the end of the hour, Judy was able to verify that the complex of buildings had been a research facility. The language code was finally being broken, and several signs had been found that simply read "Research and Development" and "Wolf River Research Park."

"What I can't understand," Paul reported, "is the high concentration of toxic chemicals in the soil up here. The small scale of these labs could hardly account for it. Presumably we're isolated from the manufacturing plant, but I found high concentrations of the remnants of a particular toxin. And only that toxin, not the soup I found below. It's a thioether derivative of a type not naturally occurring. It's so toxic that minor skin contact would give you pretty bad blisters, and breathing its vapors would probably kill you."

"I'd have to say that this had become a small village," Judy added. "We found a waste pile and even a shallow grave cemetery. I would say they lived here for several years. Finally, in perhaps one or a series of attacks, they were either driven out, killed, captured, or a combination of the three. The damage to the stockade and the fact that it wasn't rebuilt tells us that. But whatever happened, it happened sometime after the original crisis. Maybe these people had lived here because they had worked here, or because of its natural defensive position on top of this hill. It's possible that they were nomads of a sort who lived here while stripping the manufacturing plant and had always planned to move on. Or maybe it was the folks who kicked them out that stripped the place. Based on disturbances in the detritus strata, most of the material was scavenged before the stockade was compromised. Regardless, I would say that they came under attack and that the stockade was breached by both ramming and fire, that it was not rebuilt, and the village was abandoned."

Reggie reported to the *Cuddy* that they had found indications of warfare but that the violence had occurred after the planet was already in decay. He described the toxic chemicals they found and reported they were probably not the causation factor they were looking for, because they had been found only in limited areas.

Making their way back into the woods, they put some distance between themselves and the morbid desolation of the chemical facility and then made camp for the night. They made no fires. They slept in a containment tent, guarded by motion and infrared detectors. They awoke just before dawn, ate a breakfast of chemically heated rations, and began their march toward the village shortly after dawn. They followed the general course of the river and stayed off the game trails. They kept to the deep woods, moving carefully, wanting to see before being seen. Occasionally they would turn in toward the river and quietly sit and watch for signs of intelligent life. They began to see more wildlife—some deerlike creatures as well as small game similar to rabbits, squirrels, and birds.

They had a lunch of liquid nutrients passed through the tube connections into their helmets and then started the last leg of their march to the village. In midafternoon, they came to a bluff overlooking the confluence of the two streams that made up the river they had been following. Below them on the far side of the river, they could see a village nestled inside the Y formed by the junction of the two waterways. It sat on a broad, level shelf just above the floodplain. Below it, on the shelf of the floodplain itself, stood a sixty-acre field of cultivated crops. A small orchard lay to the right end of the field. Above the village, a moderate slope led fifty meters up to a forested plateau.

The village was made up mostly of some twenty dilapidated log cabins, plus several old tents and open campfires. A large two-story stone building sat at the center rear of the village. Three canoes lay on the near side of the river where they had been beached and pulled ashore. Tall, green crops laid out in straight rows were being tended in the fields by twelve men, women, and children. They appeared to be weeding it and using hand pumps to spray some sort of substance on the crops. Mark supposed that they were spraying nutrients or insecticides. A similar group of five people were down at the riverbank washing clothes. At what looked like a barn, a group of five men were tending two horselike animals and repairing a four-wheeled wagon. Next to the barn, three older boys were leading two ox-like animals in the never-ending orbits of an ox-powered flour mill.

Mark set up a directional microphone and video receiver so that he could hear and record the conversations at the village. When the *Cutty* passed overhead in its regular orbit, he would upload the data—complete audio with a contemporaneous visual record—to the *Cutty Sark*'s main computer, just as had been done with the signs at the chemical plant. More capable than what they had in the exoanthropology kit, its linguistic/cryptoanalysis program would soon be fully translating the alien language. After positioning the surveillance equipment, the astronauts moved back into the deep woods and established a simple base camp. They lived and worked in the containment tent, never leaving the secluded camp, so as not to risk detection. They watched and listened at their monitors as the mechanical eavesdroppers recorded the village's daily routine for analysis by the *Cutty*'s main computer. They maintained this routine for four boring days.

Elizabeth was using the new science equipment at the lander to determine what the consequences would be if the earth's and alien's biologics came into contact with one another. As was usually the case, the two biological systems were so different that contamination would not be a problem. However, to be absolutely certain that they could not contaminate the humanoids, and to further study the cause of the planet's problems, Elizabeth knew she would have to have a sample of their tissue. She radioed her request to Reggie.

On the evening of their seventeenth day, Reggie and Mark made preparations for obtaining a tissue sample. First, having learned that the aliens seldom traveled at night, the two astronauts were going to use the opportunity this presented to place some additional surveillance cameras along a trail that followed the nearest of the two streams leading to the village. Traders and hunters frequently used the trail, and there were often a few stragglers still on the trail at day's end. The two crewmen made their way to the trail, positioned their equipment, and, well before dawn, made their way back to the base camp. That day, they slept. In midafternoon, they made their way to a ridge overlooking the trail where they had set up the new surveillance equipment. They waited until twilight before working their way closer to the trail. Traffic would be moving just one way now—toward the village. With the equipment they had placed the previous night, Reggie was able to use a handheld receiver to safely survey a two-kilometer stretch of the trail. They were able to keep moving and yet could stop and get well hidden if need be. At the midpoint of this monitored section, they settled into a new position barely thirty meters from the trail. Twilight was turning to dark when the monitor showed two alien travelers entering the trap. Reggie continued to monitor both ends of the trail, anxiously hoping that no additional travelers would appear. There was a limit to how many they could handle. What they really needed was an isolated target if the equipment and plan were to work properly.

Having selected the target, the two Earthmen now moved closer to the trail. Just fifteen meters from its edge, they stopped, set up a synaptic scrambler, draped it and themselves with camouflage netting, and sat back to watch the monitor. They soon saw the two aliens turn a bend just one hundred meters down the trail and come into view. The scrambler was part of the exoanthropologist's equipment, so Reggie merely observed while Mark switched it on and went to work. While rotating the controls through the entire spectrum (except for the window cut through the human spectrum), Mark watched for the signs of feedback distortion indicating that the correct frequency was being broadcast. When the signal spiked, he slowly increased the power at that frequency and watched for physical responses in the targets' behaviors. Mark had said that he had his doubts. They were operating at the field unit's maximum range for most conscious humanoid species, and they could not be sure it would even work on this race of aliens.

Turning to the monitor, Reggie could now clearly hear as well as see the two targets talking and clumsily making their way along the trail; they did not appear to be woodsmen. They moved closer and closer to Reggie's position, completely unaware of the impulses that were beginning to scramble their thought and memory processes. The two Earthmen, with Mark making minor adjustments to his equipment, patiently waited, still unsure that the scrambler would work. The targets gradually passed into close range of the scrambler field. They continued walking normally, stumbled once, then again, and then momentarily stood motionless before slumping to the ground unconscious. The two Earthmen ran quickly forward—one to each fallen target. They inserted long hypodermic needles into the limp bodies and extracted tissue samples while simultaneously administering a local anesthetic. Then they quickly checked what was being carried in the travelers' heavy backpacks. Besides personal items, all they found were rolls of very old used electrical wire and antique light switches. Their work finished, the two astronauts covered their tracks as they backed away from the site and went into hiding to keep watch over the aliens until they awakened and resumed their journey. Only then did the astronauts pack up the scrambler and the camouflage netting and cautiously make their way back to base camp. The carefully hidden surveillance cameras remained. Upon returning to camp, the tissue samples were picked up by the aero droid. The sample would be delivered to Elizabeth for analysis within the hour.

Awakening slowly from their stupor, the two victims continued on their journey. Like two drunks still in a haze, they managed to stand and somehow begin walking, although their senses were far from being fully recovered. Also like drunks, they were left with no memories of the events that had transpired. They did not remember the tingling sensation precursing the numbness that had overtaken them as the signals going through the synapses of their brains had been slowly scrambled. They did not remember the fog and the blinding white light—the optical illusions caused by the misfires in their optic nerves as the scrambler began to do its work. They did not remember the feeling of helpless floating. Nor did they remember becoming so lightheaded that they fell unconscious to the ground. They would never remember the biopsies or the trouble they had getting up and walking. Instead, they were left only with vague impressions of fear and confusion. It was something neither man talked about. With no specific memories, each attributed his apprehension to his fear of the darkening forest. The event had become a dream, forgotten upon awakening.

CHAPTER 5

The Agricultural Village

Twenty-five days had elapsed since the landing. The biologic containment studies were largely complete. Elizabeth confirmed that the generic decontamination, vaccines, and receptor blockers were sufficient to protect the astronauts and the planet from one another, so the containment suits could be set aside. At last they could work without the clear bucket helmets and liquid diets. Mark had finished their costumes, a good bank of linguistic information had been fed into the computers, and the settings at which the scrambler had worked were fed into the stun guns and personal issue scramblers. All was ready for first contact. Reggie decided that he and Mark would go into the village while Judy and Paul would stay hidden and serve as their backup.

The clothing and equipment Mark had prepared for the four of them were similar to that worn by the aliens they had seen on the trail. The astronauts now wore crudely made boots or moccasins, brown wool pants, and brown suede leggings that went to the tops of their thighs. The leggings laced in the front from the top to the shins. They wore loose-fitting, rust-brown, flax tunics that hung to midthigh. The tunic had five large buttons up the front, the top three of which were, they had seen, left unbuttoned in hot weather. The tunics had elbow-length sleeves.

Around their waists over the tunics, they wore wide leather belts with pouches for flints, trail bread, and other small items, including a compass and simple matches. Hidden in one pouch, Reggie carried a monitor for the surveillance cameras. A leather scabbard attached to the belt held a dagger with a two-foot blade. Each man carried a pack on his back with trade goods and camping equipment. Unlike the aliens, each man carried, hidden in the bottom of his backpack but accessed from underneath, communications and sampling equipment. Over their packs, they wore dark blue, almost black, woolen capes with hoods that could be raised to protect their heads from inclement weather. Also unlike the aliens, hidden in the capes' linings were personal-issue scramblers and hidden pouches for a stun gun and night-vision glasses.

The trade goods would help them in their deception and also help them acquire any aid they would need in the alien society. They carried coils of wire and electrical switches taken from the lifeboat that were similar to the ones they had found on the aliens. These had been flown in later by several trips of the same miniature aero droid that Elizabeth had used to retrieve the tissue samples. It was Mark's guess that the aliens carried these items for trade. They also packed a few mess kits, an ax, fishhooks, and fishing line from their survival kits. Mark believed that these would also be good trade items. He explained that most simple societies have a need for such cookware and simple tools.

The capes could be rolled up and stored in their backpacks in warm weather, but in the predawn dampness and chill of the beginning of their twenty-sixth day, the cloaks helped them keep warm. Reggie and Mark said good-bye to Judy and Paul, put on their night-vision glasses, and headed toward the monitored section of the trail.

The plan was to enter the trail without being seen and then hike into the village as any trader would. They got to the valley just before dawn, verified by monitor that there was no one else on the trail, and then carefully made their way down into the valley and onto the trail. There, they stopped and rested before starting the final leg of their journey. As the last star disappeared from the morning sky, they removed their night goggles, stood up, stretched, and headed toward the village.

Almost three hours later, they could see the village through the trees, on the far side of the sleepy river. To cross the river, they borrowed one of the canoes beached on the near side. They had seen others do this and hoped that the canoes were communal.

As they paddled across the slow-moving waterway, they had some idea of what to expect in the alien village. They had watched and listened on monitors for almost a week. But they still felt great apprehension as the canoe struck the bank and Mark jumped out from the front and began pulling the boat ashore, followed by Reggie from the stern.

The village was well into its daily routine. Most of the villagers were working in the fields. They were dressed the same as the traders except that they wore neither leggings nor capes. The two astronauts headed toward the large stone building at the rear center of the village. That was where visitors first seemed to go. The villagers they passed diverted their eyes and said nothing to them. The two Earthmen looked toward but then basically ignored them, as they had seen on their monitors other visitors do. As they walked past the cabins and tents that constituted the village's housing, they could see that many of the villagers were still sleeping or just sitting or lying about. Fully a third of the tents were so badly tattered that they obviously did little but ease the force of the wind. The cabins were little better. Two of them had caught fire and been only partially repaired. All of the cabins were in a state of disrepair, with holed roofs, doors broken or nonexistent, broken glass in the windows, and in general, looked to be barely inhabitable.

Mark believed that the large stone building they were heading for was some kind of trading or civic center. It was centrally located on the higher ground of the slope at the far end of the village. The stone and gravel path that they were following ran from the top of the riverbank through the field and the center of the village to its front door. The building was a full two stories high, had a gabled roof, and was about thirty-three meters long. But it too was in disrepair. The front door had apparently rotted off its hinges and what was left of it leaned against the wall next to the dark opening that led inside. A villager who was just coming out lowered his head and stepped out of the astronauts' path as they reached the door and stepped into the coolness of the dark and musty building.

The doorway led through the building's thick stone wall into a large room that took up the center half of the ground floor. Smaller rooms each took up one-fourth of the building at each end. Against the end walls of the center room, staircases led to the second floor. The floor was made of broad wooden planks. Parts of it were rotted out, and the astronauts had to step around unguarded holes. Larger holes were covered apparently with whatever material was most immediately convenient when required. A rudimentary bar ran in front of the stairs to the right. Five small tables, each with four chairs, sat at that end in front of the bar. The left end of the room had a service counter, scales, and half-empty shelves along the wall, holding pots, knives, rope, clothing, and other items displayed for trading.

The surveillance equipment had allowed the astronauts to see inside the building, but the distance was too great for the somewhat limited field equipment to allow them to hear inside. And without total 360-degree surveillance, it was impossible for the computer to lip-read. So although Reggie and Mark knew the basic layout of the building, they could not be certain of how to interact with its occupants.

The astronauts hesitated while their senses adjusted to the dark and musty room. They knew that visitors first went to the bar, so they headed there first. However, they could not drink. With incomplete knowledge of the alien customs and biology, they could not be certain that what the aliens routinely drank would not be poisonous to humans. Instead, Mark began to investigate by questioning the bartender.

"Do you trade?" he asked.

"Yes, sir, at your convenience, sir. Are there particular items you desire? Have a drink or food first, sir?"

Mark uttered a curt no and asked to see the store's trade goods. They were led to the shop at the far end. The shopkeeper continued.

"We have the best whiskey. Also, we have knives, spear points, grain, rope, and trail bread. We have medicinal herbs and salt."

"Your shelves look very empty."

"Forgive us, but our village does not supply as many goods as it once did. But we do have some quality goods to trade from the Hill People. We have a compass, good reliable matches in a waterproof box, this telescope (good for hunting game or watching for enemies), this fluid for helping start a fire in damp wood, and ..." he brought out a box from under the counter, "these six gas bombs. They burn the eyes and lungs. Breathing it will kill. It is a very good weapon."

The two Earthmen's eyes briefly met, and then Reggie turned back to the shopkeeper. "You have gas bombs?"

"Yes, sir, a very good gas. Just ten measures of wire for one canister—and just one is sufficient, depending of course on the wind and directions of attack."

Reggie requested more information about what the gas was made of and how it worked, but the shopkeeper explained that he was only a merchant and knew nothing more. He said that his village was peaceful and that he knew only what he had been told and had never even seen the gas used. Reggie put the wire he had on the table but learned he did not have enough to buy a sample.

Reggie spread the rest of his goods on the counter. "As you can see, we have some fine fishing equipment, sewing needles, thread, knives with good strong blades, a very good ax, and equally good cooking tools." He placed samples on the table for inspection.

"I can trade the gas for none of these," the alien responded. I trade the gas for the Hill People. And they allow me to trade it only for wire, electrical supplies, chemicals, and such. Please take no offense. I could use another customer. Only the Vikmoor and a very few other traders come in with the quality of goods that you have. They can be bad people but are good traders. Try to get more wire. Do you need rope? What about spear points or salt? I can also give you much whiskey for any of these goods."

"No, but I will give you one of the knives and this set of cooking gear for a compass, telescope, match, and fire-starting fluid." Reggie wanted to continue to deepen the relationship as well as study the technology.

"Very good. Very good choices." The shopkeeper took the knife and a mess kit and turned the bartered for goods over to Reggie. "Perhaps if other traders come, they will trade you something for the ax. It is a very fine tool."

"We will see," Reggie answered as he turned around and tested the compass's bearing-finding ability. The pointer was mounted in a dampening fluid and gave a quick and steady bearing. "Very good. You say someone else made these? The Hill People? Who are they? And who are the Vikmoor?"

"The Hill People? You don't know about the Hill People?" His manner became cautious. As little as the Earthman knew of the villagers, he could still sense the shopkeeper's apprehensive body language and voice tone. "Where are you from?"

"Never mind." Reggie decided to ask, and risk being asked, no further questions. "We will stay and eat."

Reggie and Mark walked across to one of the tables and sat down, swinging their packs to the ground. Because they still preferred not risking eating the alien food, they reached into their packs and brought out their own provisions. They had packed plain-looking containers that would raise no suspicion. They each unwrapped a small loaf of protein bread the consistency of traditional fruitcake. They broke off pieces and ate, washing the dry protein loaf down with vitamin juice from glass jars that were similar to those used by the men they had intercepted on the trail.

Reggie handed the compass over to Mark and began studying the telescope. "I can't say much against this compass, and they did a nice job on this telescope." He turned and faced one of the windows and pointed the instrument across the village commons to the far shore. "It has a firm fit and good optics." He scanned the far shore. "It looks like we're about to get company. Two more traders are headed this way." He handed the telescope to Mark. Two traders were climbing into one of the remaining canoes on the opposite bank and were no doubt headed for the village. "I don't want to take any chances. I'm going to set my scrambler to 'burst,' just in case."

"Better raise your hood," suggested Mark, who was more familiar with the equipment. "At this range and power level, there might be some spillover; the settings were pretty close to human, and I've seen people dropped to their knees by these things even when they weren't."

With just a pull on a ring inside the lieutenant's cloak, the scrambler would send out one burst of energy in a 360-degree field that in the short range afforded inside the tavern would drop their victims unconscious. It would not be the elegant, unremembered event as was the carefully orchestrated episode on the trail, and it would not last long, but it would give the Earthmen time to escape. The insulation in their own hoods would keep them safe from it. Reggie knew he could simply leave, but he wanted to find out as much as he could about the village and wanted to risk staying. They still needed clues to determine exactly what had happened to set the planet's technological and presumably its sociological clocks back in time, and the village was a good place to get them. Without learning what had happened to the planet, there was just too great a chance of carrying something back to the *Cutty*. Besides, it was the scientific mission of the *Cutty Sark* to investigate anything new and different. And the situation here qualified as that.

They could hear and trace the footsteps of the two alien visitors crunching across the gravel, up the wooden steps, through the open door, and into the center of the big room. Wordlessly, the aliens plodded across the wood floor, their footsteps echoing hollowly beneath them, not stopping until they reached the bar. They demanded "strong drink" and leaned with their backs against the bar, facing the two Earthmen. Neither party greeted the other. The two newcomers gulped down their drinks and slammed their empty glasses down on the bar. After a short time, the taller of the two aliens, the one to the left, loudly addressed his partner, obviously intending to be loud enough that everyone in the room could hear.

"Well, Bodolf, we've been here for almost a full minute, and these two children have yet to provide us drink. Perhaps they need to be taught manners."

"Yes, Gruff, I'll teach them their lesson for you."

Reggie spoke up. "Barkeeper, provide these visitors with ale. We'll trade you for it before we leave." He continued to stare straight ahead, at his own table of food and drink. "We apologize. We are new here."

"Good enough. Bartender, ale for me and my friend and a round for our new friends."

The two aliens helped themselves to seats at the Earthmen's table. "You are strangers here. Where are you from?" Gruff asked.

"Almost a full month's journey. We come from a valley at the far side of the long lake. We came to see if there is trade here," Reggie told them.

"The villagers here are weak," the other alien offered. "The trade here is poor. It provides little food and poor weapons, but it does have the salt we need. I know a village that will trade meat for salt, and there is little meat left anywhere. I have traded there for many years. But I hear that the Vikmoor just found them. I hear that the villagers fell into a mobbed frenzy and resisted the Vikmoor thieves, but they were helpless against the Hill People's gas that the Vikmoor now use. Many died from the gas. Many more died later from the hatred burning within them. More will die if the Vikmoor return and take much more of their feed grain. They took as much as they could carry with their first raid. And of course they butchered as much cattle as they could carry. But there is a rumor that more cattle were up in the hills, grazing. I will trade the last of the gold coins my father's father gave me for any beef I can get. If I cannot trade there, I know a village where I can trade for dried apples. That is what it is like here."

The two aliens returned to the bar. "Prepare two more ales."

The barkeeper nervously filled the two aliens' glasses. "Will that be all, sir? Shall I show you to a room, sir?"

"No. I know the way. Just give me a key," said Gruff's partner. He turned to Reggie. "These people are all afraid of us. They think we are all like the Vikmoor." With that, he downed his drink and headed up the stairs to the right. Gruff downed his own glass of ale, grabbed a bottle of whiskey, and slumped into a chair at one of the other tables. He sat glaring at the two Earthmen and continued his drinking.

Reggie turned to Mark. "Let's go out and look around the village. We'll stay the night and see what develops in the morning."

They got up from the table and walked outside. Reggie continued, "I'm curious about who these Hill People are. The technology is higher than what these villagers have. Is wire the only metal they trade for? What is it needed for? Why is this village so dilapidated? And does any of it relate to what set this planet back?"

The afternoon was spent walking through the village. First, they walked over to the barn and blacksmith shop where they had seen the wagon being worked on when they had first spied on the village with their surveillance equipment. The unrepaired wagon still sat there. Its large, simple wheels were simply several wooden planks cut to form a large circle and joined together by cross members. One wheel had a broken cross member. A long timber pole lying next to the wagon indicated that workmen had tried to rig a lever so that they could raise the wagon and remove the wheel, but they obviously had not finished. The astronauts next inspected the mill and the grain storage barn. The barn was nearly empty, which was not surprising considering the season, but the village obviously had low reserves. The barn itself was in poor repair. Its roof had large gaping holes that had been patched only with sheets of canvas, but even the canvas had worn out and flapped in the breeze. In the back of the village, next to a brine spring, several iron caldrons full of the spring water had been hung from tripods over open fires so that the salt could be boiled out. One caldron sat waiting to have its salt scraped out. An adjacent shed held a small inventory of sacks of salt and additional caldrons. Three villagers were busy cutting wood and tending the fires, but most of the caldrons had gone cold and rusty from nonuse.

It was midafternoon by the time the astronauts made their way into the agricultural field. As observed earlier, several villagers appeared to be weeding, while others applied some sort of spray substance. The villagers kept working and only looked at the two Earthmen out of the corner of their eyes. Mark walked up to one of the young men doing the spraying, asked him what it was for, and was told it was for killing insects.

Mark asked how it was made and was told that the villagers traded the Hill People for it.

"They come here several times a year. We trade salt and grain for it. Just like we trade for the other things we need. We used to trade meat also, but that is something we no longer have." The farmer would not let his eyes meet Reggie's. Reggie thought the farmer seemed hesitant to talk but even more hesitant to refuse.

"Where do they come from?" Reggie asked.

"We do not know, only that they come from that way." He pointed to the north along the river and up into thickening foothills.

"They trade with others for other things. But no one knows where their village is. They keep themselves hidden. They leave their goods here, and the shopkeeper trades for them. Some of their goods get stolen by the Vikmoor, but most of the traders will not steal the Hill People's goods because they are afraid of them."

"But who are these Vikmoor?" Reggie persisted.

"Another village. Up the other river. A week's journey from here. They come and take our food, women, and whatever else they need."

"You cannot stop them?"

"You mean resist sharing? We are a religious and peaceful people. No one may set himself above another. To fight is to give in and become one of them, to let your feelings become slave to them. That is what destroyed the old cities."

"What happened to them?"

The alien hesitated. Reggie guessed that he was wondering why he was being asked so many questions that probably had, to the alien, either obvious answers or were just as obviously unanswerable. But the alien was timid enough that he automatically did his best to answer. "The old ones had their magic taken from them by the gods when they used it in war." His eyes still had not met Reggie's.

Now he was looking off to the side and just staring across the field. "The gods stretched out their hands and took the magic away. Without the magic, the cities became dark, water no longer flowed, the cities died." The alien looked up suspiciously at the strangers.

"Who leads this village?" Reggie changed the subject.

"We all do. We have a village meeting at every moon cycle. We talk. We agree. We plan."

"What about a religious leader, a priest?"

"We had a priest, but he died not long ago. It was shortly after a Vikmoor visit. They took his sacred relics because of the gold and silver in them. He lost himself to his anger. He wanted us to prepare weapons and go out to fight the Vikmoor. He was very angry. It was all he talked about. Instead of sharing with the Vikmoor, he put himself first. He lost his soul, became sick, and died.

"I do not understand. Why do you ask me these things?" The questioning was beginning to exasperate the young man.

"We come from far away. We came to trade. What can you tell us about the Hill People?"

"Little. They bring goods to trade. Every month, two or three of them come to the trading post. They leave goods and pick up goods. Sometimes they trade for village goods; sometimes they trade for things left by other traders. They bring us medicine to protect our crops and animals, and medicines for our people. We give them food or the wire or other things we got by trading with others." He spoke as he went back to work.

"Why is the village in such poor condition?" Reggie asked.

"Oh, this is just temporary. Everyone is comfortable. We have shelter enough for all who need it. Those who cannot have cabins have tents. Things are good enough for now, but I admit we need to start some repairs. Perhaps when we finish in the fields today, we could spend some time on the cabins. But first we will have to have a meeting and decide whose cabin to repair first. Of course, no one will ask to have their own repaired. And I'm not sure who will ask for them. That would look like trying to be boss and putting yourself above others. It gets very difficult. I'll wait and see what happens at the next meeting."

With that, the alien turned from them and pretended to concentrate more fully on his work. Reggie and Mark moved to the edge of the field.

"Lieutenant," Mark began, "I want you to take a look at these crops. There aren't many weeds where they're working. Unless they grow incredibly fast, which we've seen no sign of, this daily weeding by all these people is a waste of manpower. And there sure are plenty of other things that need to be done."

"Agreed. They need to get organized. Let's go back to the trading post."

It was late afternoon when the two Earthmen returned to the building that they had learned was called the "trading post." The shorter of the two traders they had met earlier, Gruff, was still there. The room was empty except for him and the barkeeper/shopkeeper. No additional traders had arrived.

"A poor time for trade," Reggie commented to Gruff as he approached Gruff's table. Mark sat at a table farthest in the bar area from Gruff's. Reggie sat down with Gruff.

"Gruff, I'd like to trade for some of the Hill People's goods, but I'm short of wire. I'd like to make you a deal." Reggie placed the survival ax, a survival knife, sewing needles, thread, a mess kit, and several fishing hooks and line on the table. He also put out the compass and telescope that he had traded for earlier. "I'll trade you all of these things for the five measures of wire I need."

"I need none of those things. The small amount of wire I have I will trade here myself for food. Perhaps my partner, Bodolf, will trade with you, but I don't expect to see him until tonight. He is resting for the festival."

"Festival?"

"Tonight's marriage festival."

Mark had overheard the conversation, and the exoanthropologist in him could not resist interrupting. "Excuse me, Gruff, but we're new here. What's this festival about?"

"The women choose a husband. They do this every season. A dusk-to-dawn festival. Much food and drink. Go to sleep until you hear the drums. Then you will see." With that, he stood up, downed his whiskey, and headed upstairs.

Reggie turned to his partner. "The *Cutty*'s due overhead. Let's report in. We'll find a discreet place where we can use the radio. Then I'm sure the exoanthropologist in you will want to see this festival."

They walked down to the river and along the bank until they were out of sight of the village. Then Reggie pulled a billfold-sized package out of an inner breast pocket. He pulled out the six-inch antenna, turned the selector switch to G2 for his group's ground channel, and pushed the call button. Mark concentrated on keeping on the lookout for intruders.

At the surveillance camp, Judy and Paul's communicators began to softly beep. Judy had been watching Reggie and Mark's progress on the monitors and answered before the third beep. "Hello, Lieutenant. Having fun?"

"Loads. We're going to a party tonight. What's news?"

"Nothing here, Lieutenant. No contact with the locals. Jake says that he and Eric have made some real progress on the lander. Elizabeth wants more tissue samples. She'd really like to do a complete physical on one of these people."

"What's new from the *Cutty*?"

"Nothing that I've heard. I'll patch them in. Stand by." She punched another button, and the radio went briefly silent. A few moments later, it squawked with the sound of static, followed by the voice of Captain Connors.

"Hello, Lieutenant. Any problems?"

"No, sir, but we have made contact." He explained what they had seen and learned. "Anything new on your end?"

"Not yet, but we're still pretty sure it was a particle beam device of some kind that hit you. We dipped down twice with a lifeboat to try to draw it out and put a fix on it, but it must be pretty well camouflaged. We can't even isolate its radar transmitters. They seem to shut off and switch to a series of secondary units. We can't isolate any single one. If it was a weapon that hit you, I'm afraid that it may eventually be trained on us, so I don't want to chance attracting its attention by sending down anything else just yet. I do have one big bit of information for you. We've been trying to confirm and locate that nuclear power plant I told you about by studying the local magnetic fields, and it looks like you're real close to it. We still can't pinpoint it—it may have more than just natural shielding hiding it—but it seems to be just to the north of you."

"That's in the same direction as that Hill People village. We'll try to make contact with them next."

"We've got some photos that do show some villages in that area. I'll transmit them down."

"Great. I'll get back to you then."

Reggie outlined a plan for returning to the surveillance camp in the morning and signed off. Then he and Mark returned to the trading post and got a room for the night. It was Spartan, with two bunks, a simple but sturdy wooden table with two chairs, and a large, heavy trunk with a lock in which they could store their goods and gear. There was a washbasin but no running water. They learned that servants brought up water in buckets. Waste was removed the same way. They ate from their rations and lay down to rest.

They were awakened by the sounds of drums and loud voices in the commons. It was well past dusk. In the center of the commons, a large bonfire blazed. The astronauts went down to investigate.

Many of the villagers were obviously intoxicated. Others were feasting on a scrawny ox-like animal that had been slaughtered and set out to roast over a fire. It was the most laughter and play the Earthmen had seen there. Some of the older men and women had formed a band consisting of hollow log drums, flutelike instruments, and a large five-stringed instrument that looked something like a harp but sounded more like a plucked guitar. The band was heavy with percussion. The young men of the village were dressed in colorful and elaborate costumes. They wore clean leggings and jackets, and capes colored bright red. The jackets were pulled tight and narrow at the waist and were broad and padded at the shoulders, highlighting the young men's figures. They wore elaborately handcrafted necklaces and ankle chains. Some of them had their hoods up, and seeing the red peaked hoods and red capes, Reggie was reminded of the colorful red-feathered cardinals of his home state of Indiana, and for the first time in his space career, he was homesick.

Because he had seen no one in the village wearing it before, Reggie was surprised to see that some of the young men were also wearing colorful facial makeup. Their lips were darkened with an almost black stain, which highlighted the whiteness of their teeth. A stain applied to the cheeks added color to the complexions of even those who did not work in the fields. Everyone was eating and drinking. Soon the young men began to fall into small groups and dance. These groups slowly merged one by one until there was one long dance line. The dancers pulled back their shoulders, stuck out their chests, and, pulling their knees high, pranced from side to side in rhythmic unison. Suddenly, one of the women ran forward and grabbed one of the men and pulled him from the line. She gave him a piece of bread, and they joined other couples who were helping the drums pound out the rhythm of the dance. Soon, most of the men had been taken from the line. Those remaining soon tired of the dance and once again broke into small groups, which also soon dissolved.

Drink was raised in toast to what the astronauts learned were newly engaged couples. Then everyone ate more and drank more. Promises were made, and dates for marriage ceremonies were set.

One of the men who had been chosen was the young man they had met in the field. Mark congratulated him.

"Thank you," he responded. "I am very fortunate. I somehow convinced Mahria that I am healthy and strong enough to be worthy of her."

The party slowly broke up. All except the unengaged young males disappeared. Their drinking and eating continued. And, judging by the relish with which Gruff and his partner consumed the remaining food and ale, the eating and drinking were a high point of the festival. Reggie and Mark returned to their bunks. After getting some sleep, they planned to return to the surveillance camp. It was the end of their twenty-sixth day on the planet.

CHAPTER 6

The Search

In a meeting called by Connors aboard the *Cutty Sark*, the researchers summarized the minimal progress toward discovering what had happened to the planet. It was known that its life-forms were carbon based and that the botanical life cycles seemed to be on par with those of Earth's. No accelerated growth had been discovered to account for the way the planet was overgrown, so it did not appear that the plants caused the apocalypse. Also, radar imaging of the planet's ocean and polar regions had been added to the scans of the visible surface and had still uncovered no cratering indicative of a comet or asteroid collision. Core sample data transmitted from the landing party showed no indications of significant climate or weather changes. Tree growth rings were consistent with normal growth patterns. Higher than normal radiation levels had been detected, but they were so low that global nuclear warfare could be ruled out. Conventional warfare seemed unlikely due to the general absence of attributable destruction. But chemical and biological warfare had yet to be ruled out. Archeological evidence of mass graves or traces of chemical or biologic toxins on the scale sufficient to account for the planet's condition had yet to be found but were still a possibility. And the evidence did indicate that the cities had been in physical decay for as much as one hundred years. It would be up to the shore party to obtain additional data.

Reggie decided that after a day of resting at the surveillance camp, he would take Paul on the expedition to return to the village for more studies and to attempt to locate and contact the Hill People. Judy and Mark would follow. He thought he might need Paul's science background, and he wanted Judy to move into the village so that she could obtain more biopsies for Elizabeth. Getting biopsies from a wider range of subjects was the next logical step in the science survey. By pairing Mark with Judy and himself with Paul, there would be one experienced person in each contact team. He would have Judy and Mark wait three days before heading for the village themselves. His plan was to go back to the village to try again to get more information and advice about finding the Hill People and did not want to overwhelm the villagers and traders and put them on their guard. He hoped to be gone by the time they got there. This distribution would stretch his personnel thin. Neither contact party would have backup. There would be no one in position to observe progress and, if necessary, extract an endangered team. This was a violation of protocol, but with his limited number of personnel, Reggie had no choice. At least he would have an experienced person on each team. He also knew that the *Cutty* could regularly monitor them from orbit.

Early the next morning, Reggie and Paul hiked to the village for a day of collecting environmental samples and trying to find out more about the Hill People. Gruff and his partner were gone. The astronauts spent the morning collecting water samples from the river and soil samples from the agricultural fields and the commons. In the afternoon, they obtained air and material samples from in and around some of the buildings and tents, including some of the cabins, the barn, and the trading post.

In the late afternoon, they returned to the trading post to get a room for the night. Several unfamiliar traders had arrived since that morning. Two were drinking. Two were arm wrestling. Three others were eating. The room became momentarily quiet as the two Earthmen entered and took an isolated table at the far corner of the room. The astronauts removed some food from their backpacks and started eating. They hoped to overhear information about the Hill People or evidence of warfare, plagues, or other causes of the planet's problems.

Reggie and Paul had just started eating when Gruff and his partner returned. Gruff's face was caked with dust and dirt, and to Reggie he looked as if he had lost a lot of weight. As he walked, he lifted his legs like they were tubes of sand, and he leaned heavily onto the spear that he now used as a walking stick. His face showed no emotion.

Then Gruff stopped. His eyes met Reggie's, and suddenly the alien just stood and stared at the Earthman. A grin slowly spread across his face. Reggie began to feel uneasy. He knew that in some cultures showing teeth could just as easily be a threat as it could be a sign of good humor. He was afraid this might be the former. Despite the grin, the rest of Gruff's face showed no sign of good cheer. And then Reggie realized the face was no longer emotionless. The eyes narrowed, and Gruff's facial muscles were pulling tight. Desperation had turned Gruff into an animal on the hunt.

Slowly, Gruff took one halting short step toward Reggie's table. Then he hesitated for a second before walking all the way around behind Reggie, circling the table, and stopping and standing behind him. He shifted his spear to his left hand and grasped the hilt of his long knife with his right hand. Bodolf at first stayed where he was. No words were exchanged between them. But by the time Gruff stood standing behind Reggie, Bodolf was standing directly in front of them, not a meter from their table, and his hand too moved up to grasp the hilt of his knife. Perceiving the danger, Reggie raised his hood and furtively prepared to engage his synaptic scrambler. There was no time to warn Paul, who was not trained for contact and did not pick up the hint. This meant that Reggie would have to set off the scrambler and deal with Paul if he got knocked down. Reggie waited, hoping Gruff's display was just territorial posturing. The astronauts had never seen traders actually attack anyone. But Gruff's intentions soon proved to be more than posturing.

"What do you have to trade?" Gruff asked as he slid his knife out of its sheath.

Reggie sat motionless. He did not turn to face Gruff. "Gruff, what are you doing? You don't plan on stealing my goods, do you?"

"My family is hungry. We must do what we must do."

At least this exchange gave Paul the time to realize why Reggie had raised his hood and raised his own.

"What's happened, Gruff? What's wrong?" Reggie asked as he reached down for his bag of goods.

"I have lived in the forest. The strong survive, and the weak die. That is the way it is in the forest and the way it is in trading. The smartest trader or the trader with the most goods to trade survives. The others do not. Hunting and trading are the same. What difference does it make if Bodolf trades away the last of the gold coins he was given by his father's father, or if I use the strength and weapons I received from my father and take what I need? Either way, we get the goods so that we may live, but others shall go hungry or may lose their wives because they cannot provide for them."

"One is stealing, and the other is not. Sit down, Gruff. We will give you our goods." Gruff remained standing.

"Hunting is hunting. There is nothing personal about it," Gruff went on. "The strong survive. The rules are the same. There is no such thing as stealing. You would just have me not use all of my skills."

Reggie had not yet decided whether to actually help Gruff or to trigger the scrambler.

"Every village I have been to has been the same," Gruff continued. "They each had poor crops, had already traded them away, or had them taken by the Vikmoor. Those with anything left wanted huge amounts in trade. Even here, they are saving the last of their flour and dried fruit to trade for the Hill People's chemicals. In all of my trading, I was able to get only a few small jars of dried beef, one smoked boar shoulder, and some dried fruit. You have very good things to trade. I can use such goods to get what I need. I think I know where I can get a quarter barrel of salted beef or at least some corn flour with those goods. I do not have gold coins such as Bodolf, but the result will now be the same. Either way, some people may die simply because they cannot meet the new price or beat another's offer. I really do not see the difference. Without your goods, I am the one to die or lose my family. With them, I may not be. Such is the way of life."

"But, Gruff, men no longer live in the forest. We do not fight one another for food. We are better than that now."

"Ha. You just say that because you have the goods. I know how to use a long knife. I say the forest's rule is now the rule for me and my family. I am strong of body. That is the rule I will follow, not your rules for the weak. I have thought about it long and hard. I really do not see how I will be any worse than the Hill People. They trade their gas, knowing that the Vikmoor use it to hurt and steal. They may as well go with them on the raids."

"Gruff, I do not understand. Why did you not just take the food you wanted from the other villages or from this village?"

"I need to be welcome again. I am not as strong as the Vikmoor. And I did not think of it then, but now I have. You are a stranger here. Give me your goods."

The conflict was suddenly interrupted by shouting and the pounding footfalls of someone running toward the village from the mountains to the north. By reflex, Gruff and his partner glanced toward the commotion. Reggie and Paul quickly stood up, sidestepped them, and headed out the door. The sounds of shouting and running were coming from a young boy who, judging by the food-gathering pouch bouncing and spilling against his hip, had been out gathering berries. Reggie could tell that the boy had been running for a long time. He was gasping for breath as he frantically shouted for help over and over again, to no one in particular. He was nearly bent over, completely exhausted, as he reached the trading post. Reggie asked him what was wrong.

"A trader fell down Bald Knob! I think his leg is broken. No one else is there. He told me to just leave him. His bone is sticking out of his leg, and there is much blood! Come quick!"

"Okay, calm down. Let's go," Reggie said. They began at a fast walk, but the boy soon had his breath back and urged them to a trot. Gruff and Bodolf followed, but they were already tired and soon fell behind.

The boy led the astronauts up a U-shaped valley to the base of a thirty-meter rock cliff cut into the side of a hill by a stream that had long since meandered away. At the base of the cliff lay the injured alien. There were no signs of anyone else. "He could have a concussion, and he could go into shock," Paul guessed out loud. The injured man was breathing regularly but was barely conscious. They could see that he had a compound fracture of his lower right leg, but there were no signs of other injuries. First they used extra clothing to apply compression bandages and stopped the bleeding. Because it would soon be dark, they decided to just stabilize him and get him to the village. Reggie cut strips of material from his bedroll for more proper bandages, while Paul cut limbs from a nearby tree to make splints. Reggie laced up the bandages and splints on the broken leg. The boy stood watching while the two men used axes to begin cutting down two very small trees, the trunks of which would be used as a frame for a stretcher.

"I'd like to get out of here," Reggie said. "I expect company any time now. I sure don't like the way Gruff was acting back there." He began stripping the limbs off one of the tree trunks. Inspired by the activity, the boy took some water from his canteen and splashed it on the fallen man's face. He began to stir.

"I think he's trying to get up," the boy called out. The injured man struggled onto his elbows but then dropped back down onto his back.

Just then, Gruff and Bodolf caught up with them. The two traders came briskly walking up the same trail from the village. Each had a hand on the hilt of his long knife.

"You don't think we will let newcomers get all of these goods, do you?" asked Gruff.

The boy looked at the two Earthmen and then moved away from where the injured man lay. Reggie walked over and took his place, sat down, and began tying a cross member onto the stretcher.

"He doesn't have any goods," Reggie said while continuing his work. "See for yourself. But you can help us get him to the village. We need to clean the wound and set the break, and he needs a place to rest and get his strength back."

Gruff began rummaging around the injured man's body, searching through his clothes. Bodolf surmised from the blood the place where the victim had fallen, and the two traders looked there for anything that had been dropped. When they finished, they walked over to where Reggie was working and stood looking down at him and the injured man. Reggie stopped his work. With one hand secretly poised on his scrambler trigger and his other hand openly grasping his dagger handle, Reggie slowly stood up and faced the aliens. Paul stood off to Reggie's right in a flanking position and pulled his dagger from its scabbard—the unmistakable scraping sound signaled that the Earthman did not intend to be trifled with. The boy stepped far back, settled down on his haunches, and sat watching. The injured man groaned and began to lift his head. The two intruders turned, looked, and saw that he was coming to. They turned back to face Reggie. "You carry him where you want. He has nothing to give us for carrying him." Then they turned and headed back toward the village.

Paul moved over to the injured man. "Are you okay? Can you hear me?"

The alien nodded. "Yes," he said. But then he tried to move.

"Oh, my leg. And my head hurts."

Reggie finished the stretcher and placed it parallel to the alien's side. "But you can use your arms and legs okay?"

"Yes."

"Okay. We will try to get you to the village. Or is there somewhere else we can take you? Where is your village? You have a bad break in that leg. You need a good doctor to set it properly and clean the wound."

"I'm with a trading party. One of the others came with me to scout ahead. We were to meet the others back at our camp and come back in the morning. When I fell, there was nothing he could do, because we had no ropes or ladders, so he went for help. They should be here soon. I'll wait until they get here." With that, he lowered his head and closed his eyes. Reggie shouted for him to stay awake, slightly elevated his feet, and kept him busy with conversation. He told him where they had come from and asked if that was where he was headed.

"Ah, the village of Anaconda. Yes, that is where we are going. We go there twice a season to trade for food and whatever the other traders leave. Less comes from there now, but we get what we can."

It wasn't long before the rest of the injured man's party appeared. Advance word of its approach came from the *Cutty*, which was now passing overhead and observing the scene with its surveillance equipment. Reggie received the *Cutty*'s warning through the receiver embedded as part of the translator in his skull.

"Lieutenant Greene, you have a party of five locals approaching through the woods on that hill above you. We give them ten minutes to arrival. All of them are armed with swords. Three of them appear to also have crossbows."

Knowing little about these aliens except that they were well armed, Reggie decided to take extra precautions. He turned to the injured man. "Your friends are only a few minutes away. Be sure to let them know we are your friends. We'll move off into the woods until you say it is clear."

Reggie and Paul fell back into the woods, signaling the boy to follow them. They hid where they could not be seen from the top of the hill. Another message vibrated inside Reggie's skull. "They don't seem to be taking any precautions. They're walking right up to the cliff. You should be able to see them any second now."

Reggie called to their patient that his friends had arrived. Seconds later, their heads appeared over the edge of the cliff, and they called down. "Delmar, are you okay? We'll be right down."

"Yes, I'm okay. Three strangers have been helping me. They are friends. They are nearby. Do not harm them."

"Okay, we're coming down." A rope ladder unrolled down the side of the cliff. Then one of the armed men climbed down, and then another, who was in turn followed by two unarmed men. The remaining armed man stayed on top and pulled up the ladder. The four men gathered around Delmar while one of them checked the bandages. "They did good," he said. "Where are they?"

"Here." Reggie stepped out of the woods.

One alien stepped forward. "I am Apsel. I am the leader of this trading party. Thank you for helping Delmar. What do you want from us?"

"We want nothing. We are from a village far from here. We are here to learn and trade. This is my partner Paul, and this is the young village boy who brought us here. I am called Reggie."

"Thank you, Reggie. Now we will take my friend to the village. It will be safer there, and we have come this far, so we must try to trade."

Apsel's men helped Delmar get onto the stretcher, two of them picked it up, and then they all started toward the village. It was just past dark when they arrived. The innkeeper stirred awake and showed them to rooms. After they were settled in, Reggie and Paul went back to the injured man. He had been given fresh bandages, but nothing else had been done.

Seeing that there was no one who knew what do, and knowing that compound fractures are liable to infection that can lead to amputation and even death, Reggie decided to help the injured man as best he could. First he showed how to clean the wound using the local whiskey. And he decided to set the break himself. He asked the other traders to leave the room. "We have some secrets that we prefer to keep that way, but I promise to do no harm." The traders had some secrets of their own and saw nothing unusual in his request. They left the room.

Paul held his hand over the patient's eyes while Reggie engaged his synaptic scrambler. Then, starting at the minimum power setting, he slowly turned up the power. As their patient fell unconscious, Reggie put on his goggles, adjusted the settings until he saw a clear three-dimensional image of the break, set the broken bone, and laced up the splints. Then he doused the leg with more alcohol and bandaged it. Finally, he used his goggles to check his work and firm up the splints.

It was not until the next morning that Reggie discovered that the man they had helped was one of the Hill People. Reggie was sitting in the tavern when Apsel and his men went to the trade counter and claimed coils of wire in return for goods that had been left on consignment, and traded their insecticide for several large bags of flour and dried fruits. As Apsel's men loaded the goods into backpacks, they discussed their disappointment but lack of surprise that the available food supply was so meager. They also discussed the difficulty they would have in carrying Delmar on his stretcher in addition to the goods. Although he would have offered to help even if the traders were not Hill People, it was then that Reggie suggested that he and Paul could help by carrying either Delmar or the goods. After a long discussion within his group, Apsel announced their acceptance of the offer of help. It was shortly past noon when they left the village.

No traders were in sight as they headed back toward the cliff from where they had come. They moved quickly along the trail. At the cliff, a rope was lowered and tied in a loop under Delmar's arms. Then all seven of the men climbed to the top and joined together in pulling him up. The rope ladder was pulled up after him.

For the next hour, they traveled through woods with no trail to follow. There was little underbrush due to the thick canopy of trees. The leaves underfoot cushioned their steps as they hurried along. Apsel occasionally consulted his compass to keep them on course. There were no discernible landmarks. It was hard going, and no one talked.

At dusk, they came to a campsite that Apsel explained he and his men had prepared on their way to the trading post. They started a fire and made a meal of something that looked like pancakes. Reggie and Paul ate their own rations. The entire scene was observed from the *Cutty* whenever its orbit carried it overhead.

The two Earthmen sat huddled with the aliens around the campfire. They stared into its dancing flames and allowed it to hypnotize them into restfulness.

Apsel slowly began to speak, mostly to Reggie but partly to himself. "This has been a hard trip for us ... Delmar so badly hurt ... little wire and such poor food ... no preserved fruits and vegetables ... no meat. And some of those traders even saw part of our trail."

"Will they try to follow us?" Reggie asked.

"I do not know. Most traders stay to themselves. I have never seen them actually campaign. And I have never seen them band together. They are a very diverse lot. There is no single trader village. They come from everywhere. After all, even we are traders of a sort, but we are not the true traders. They have a certain culture of their own. They belong to no village. Most seem to like the independence and isolation of the trail itself. They keep to themselves and bother no one. Fortunately, I believe it was this type that saw where Delmar had fallen down the cliff. They know we want to be left alone and will probably not try to follow our trail."

"Why is that important to you?"

"To be left alone? To live apart from others has long been our way. We learn and share the fruits of our knowledge through our trading. But to remain hidden is our way to remain safe."

"Safe from other traders?"

"Yes."

"Especially the Vikmoor?"

"Yes. Especially the Vikmoor."

"What more can you tell me about them?"

"They have a village northeast of Anaconda. They seem to have no religion, but even traders are usually peaceful, even without religion. The Vikmoor are worse. They just take whatever they want, except from us. They seldom bother to trade. They steal. And by force if anyone resists.

Many will go hungry because of them. But they want more of our goods. They have learned that if they steal our goods from a trading post that we never leave the goods they really want there again."

Reggie needed to know more about what was going wrong with the planet. "Perhaps you can tell me what is happening at Anaconda. The village seems to be dying."

"The same thing that is happening in most villages. They are simply rotting. There is no leadership. No one seems to have the drive to get work started and finished. In my city, Poplarville, things are not so bad, but I think we have the same problem."

"Apsel, what happened? We have found ruins of great cities. Did all the cities just slowly die, like Anaconda is doing?"

"We think not. But you are lucky the priests do not hear you asking such questions. In some villages, they would gladly burn you for questioning such a thing. But my village is one of scientists. We do not fear questions. Or do you not know what the priests say? No? Then your village must be as far away as you say it is.

"The priests say that a mighty battle was fought between good and evil. They say that our knowledge and conceit expanded beyond our wisdom. In always trying to get more and more, we tried to take more from our brothers than what we each truly needed. Accumulating things showed that you were the most successful accumulator and that was the measure of success. And accumulating, indeed our whole society was at that time based on competition and survival of the strongest. It took credits to make credits, and credits were power. So, by accumulating you not only got the things you wanted, you also showed you were the strongest, the most powerful. A time came when the nations fought each other simply on the one side to expand borders, and on the other side to protect trade. We unleashed all of the power of our machines against each other to take what was really no nation's to own. Evil thus fought evil, destroying itself. But evil also nearly destroyed good. So, before that could happen, the gods destroyed our machines—the toys and weapons of our conceit. Then they sent spirits to kill the evil ones among us. The priests say that the battle between evil and good continues to this day and that that is why the gods still kill those who show anger and aggression. It will continue until all evil is destroyed."

"Is that what your people, as scientists, believe?"

"Even the scientists believe there is some truth to it. There is some truth to most all myths. Perhaps there is less evil. Most of us no longer fight to solve our problems. The gods say, 'The humble shall inherit the world,' and most of us are now more humble—others are to be put first. Those who do not, such as some of the traders and the Vikmoor, are exceptions, so you could say there is less evil in the world. We know there are remains of great cities all around us. And although no one knows exactly what happened to the cities, there are historical records that show that there was a war fought between nations. The records also show that many people simply got sick and died. It hit the soldiers first, but then it spread throughout the world. The priests claim that the gods killed all those who thought evil against their brothers. And it is a documented scientific fact that, except for the Vikmoor and a few of the traders, whoever is hateful, or whoever attacks a brother, soon becomes sick and dies."

CHAPTER 7

Poplarville

Connors sat at his command station and watched on the main view screen as the planet slowly passed beneath his ship. The quiet routine of a ship in orbit carried on around him. Except for the three men using navigational instruments to help observe the landing party, most of the activity was in the science labs. Connors had just received his ship's daily operational reports. The *Cutty Sark*'s status was unchanged. It was at 100 percent of capability. And, as reflected in the unchanging images in the view screen, the situation on the planet was also unchanged—it continued to be miserly with its secrets.

The captain contemplated all that had happened in the thirty-one days since the planet fall. A lander and its crew were stranded on the planet. The planet itself was dotted with the remains of a dead civilization, but that civilization's legacy still carried death. Something had shot down the lander and taken numerous potshots at the lifeboats. Whatever it was that had effectively destroyed the civilization could very well still be active. Reports from Greene indicated that there had indeed been a war, but except for general decay, that war was unconfirmed by physical evidence, as was the alien's claim that hatred could be terminal. Connors hoped he would know more as they gathered additional data. He could be patient a little longer. He continued to act like everything was under control—like he had seen this sort of problem a hundred times before.

Jake sat on the beach resting. The sun was setting across the lake and cast a soft pink glow across the water and onto the lander's white fuselage and wings. The spacecraft was nearly ready for flight. He and Eric had cannibalized the lifeboat's backup systems to provide the lander with the minimum instruments and controls necessary for orbital insertion and rendezvous. The lander now had docking radar, an altimeter, artificial horizon, and a simple flight computer. After first giving everything a thorough testing, the next step would be to start the VTOL system, get the lander up off the ground in a minimum hover, lower the landing skids, and drop the lander on dry ground on a wider part of the beach. Then he could patch the holes in its belly—maybe not enough for pressurization but enough to maintain aerodynamics; they could wear pressure suits into orbit if they had to. He was pushing himself as hard as he could. He presumed that *Cutty*'s scientists would soon determine how the landing party could return without getting shot down or taking a plague aboard. He wanted the lander to be ready.

Reggie stepped out of the woods and looked down on Poplarville. Apsel claimed that it was one of the few surviving cities from before the war. It lay nestled in a deep and narrow valley on the far side of a small river. What looked like well-kept houses stood to the left at the village's upriver end. Downriver stood what appeared to be a campus of utilitarian manufacturing facilities and warehouses. The houses were mostly simply made log cabins, although a few were made from flat stones mined from the riverbank. The simple construction indicated that they were probably of newer construction and not originally part of the campus. But the industrial-looking buildings were made of brick and steel and were obviously of pre-event construction. A few buildings that looked like concrete bunkers were embedded in the side of the far hill. Two dome-shaped buildings and a thirty-meter by ninety-meter slightly concave wall stood on top of that opposing hillside.

Apsel stepped up beside Reggie and explained the village's history. "The work areas were here when the war started. The gods made the machines quit working to stop the war. But not just the war machines—all of our machines. Machines had gotten us into war. We had forgotten the gods and their teachings. The machines we built were so powerful that we arrogantly thought that we controlled our own destinies. Evil took over. We were covetous, selfish, and indifferent rather than benevolent and compassionate. We showed no love for one another or for what is good. We went to war against our neighbors. We nearly destroyed each other with the power of our machines. So the gods used their spirits to destroy our machines and save us from ourselves. After the war, only the equipment in the deep bunkers still worked. Next, whether it was spirit or a plague of disease, many died. The priests say that it was our anger burning within us, that God cut down those who, after such a terrible war, could still dare harbor evil thoughts of war and revenge. There were a few who realized nothing could be done through revenge. Rather than brood on anger, they found peace in this city. They saw what needed to be done to keep our culture, our knowledge, and our history alive. As scientists, my people were used to the discipline of academics, and most worked together for the enjoyment of scientific discovery. We tried to preserve what we could of the old scientific knowledge, and what we lost, we worked to learn again. Over time, our housing was rebuilt closer to the work areas, and we built better. We did not duplicate the barracks, dormitories, and cafeterias of the old compound. We built houses for ourselves—a real city. Our community never died. We survived."

Apsel became quiet. The alien and the Earthman stood side by side. They contemplated the city that lay at their feet, its past, their pasts, and their futures.

The momentary silence was broken by two sentries stepping out of the forest from a short distance off to their left. Each sentry carried a spear and had a crossbow and arrows strapped across his back. Gas bombs and a long knife were strapped to their belts. They called for Apsel to meet them. Apsel told Reggie to wait and went to meet the sentries. Paul joined Reggie. The two Earthmen stayed where they were but could still overhear enough of the conversation to tell that Apsel had to defend the presence of the strangers.

Reggie motioned to Paul with a nod of his head toward a large, slightly concave-shaped wall structure on the far hill. "Looks like an outdoor video screen," Reggie said.

"Yeah, like that old drive-in they've got at the Detroit Auto Museum."

"I wonder what it is."

"Maybe it is a video screen. A modern version. Information could be broadcast to the whole city from there, like a big bulletin board."

"I don't think so. It has too much of an upward angle. It looks more like old-style fixed array radar. Electronically scanned type deal."

Their short discussion came to an end when one of the sentries disappeared into the woods in the direction from which he had come to "call the manager of security." Everyone else remained where they were. He returned just five minutes later. It had been agreed to allow the strangers into the city, under the condition that a sentry escort them there. Apsel motioned for Reggie and Paul to follow, and they began the hike down into the valley. The trail snaked down in long diagonal stretches, one-third of the way down into the valley at each stretch. As they descended deeper into the river valley, Poplarville disappeared from view behind the trees. It took them almost half an hour to reach the valley floor. Five more sentries awaited them there.

"I have instructions to escort Apsel and the strangers to Anton," one of them said. "Delmar is to be taken to the infirmary. My men will help the rest of you take the goods to Receiving."

A well-maintained gravel footpath led across a bridge into a clearing, past a guard shack at a gate in a three-meter-high chain-link fence, and through the residential area to the college-campus-like setting of one-, two-, and three- story flat-roofed, redbrick buildings that were part of the original compound. They were escorted to the first building, which had a sign above the door that translated to "Administration," and then led inside and through an empty central reception area, past a double door that appeared to Reggie to be an elevator door, and up a flight of stairs. There they were met by another sentry, who led them down the hall and through a single door with a placard that translated to "Director" and into a reception room containing a small desk and chair occupied by another sentry. That sentry nodded them through a door behind him to his left. This led them into a large office with a single long desk and chair facing them from in front of a large plate-glass window. The man sitting behind the desk looked up from a short stack of paperwork.

"Apsel, we are glad to see you have returned, but you must explain these two." He gestured toward the two astronauts.

Apsel introduced Anton to his two visitors and explained Delmar's accident and the help given by the Earthmen. "They asked for nothing in return—and we did need help if we were to carry both Delmar and our goods."

"What have you to say?" His eyes glanced to Paul and then fixed on Reggie.

"Our village is far from here," the lieutenant began. "We are here to trade. We are from the west, beyond the long lake."

"I am director here." The tall alien stood and began a low bow, but it was interrupted by a buzzer going off on his desk phone. He bent farther to his right, picked up the phone's handset, put it to his head, and spoke into it. "Yes." He paused, listening to the caller, but now looked toward the Earthmen and then spoke again. "They did?" Another pause, and then he looked toward Apsel. "Very well. Give him three weeks of medical absence." Then he hung up the phone. He turned again to Reggie. "That was the infirmary. They tell me you did a superb job of setting and cleaning Delmar's broken leg. That is unusual knowledge."

"I could say the same. That is the first such device I have seen for a long time, and the first I have seen that works." (He did not yet know the alien word for telephone.)

"The telephone?" (Reggie learned a new word.) "Do you have them in your village?"

"No, but we have seen many unusual things in our travels."

"Is that so? You must tell me about such things."

Reggie was concerned that too much questioning would expose the holes in their cover story, but before he had a chance to answer, Apsel interrupted them. Apsel had not guessed that Reggie was nervous, but he did not like the way the director was confronting Reggie. It was not polite, and it was beginning to appear personal. Apsel did not want the director to lose control and become angry—Anton was too good of a director, and Apsel did not want to take the chance of losing him to the sickness. Instead, Apsel decided to rescue him. "Excuse me, Anton, but we have had a very hard journey. I would like to give my friends a chance to eat and rest. They will stay with me. Could we return tomorrow?"

"Yes, of course. Rest tonight. Show your guests the Residence Compound. Come join me here tomorrow for dinner."

Apsel led them to the residential area, to a log cabin that he said was his home.

"We do not get visitors here, so we have no guest quarters. You can stay with me."

Apsel's cabin was a six-meter by fifteen-meter, rectangular, one-story building. To the left of the central door, in the far corner, the cabin was sectioned off into a three-meter by three-meter, walled bathing room. There was a similar-sized room in the front left-side corner, which they later learned was Apsel's pantry and general storage room. A square, brick stove stood in the middle of the remaining open area. A simple wood and rope bedframe with a straw mattress stood in the near corner to the right along the end wall. At the front wall to the right, up against a square window centered between the door and the end wall stood a one-meter-square wooden table with three high-backed wooden chairs, one at each open side. A single chair stood along the end wall to the left of the bed. A tall cabinet for hanging clothes and a long cabinet with three big drawers stood to the left of the chair. Glancing to his left as he entered the cabin, Reggie could see a coat and hat hung from a hook on the wall beside the door. Several oil lamps hung on the walls, but there were no paintings, pictures, or other ornamentation. A shuttered window was cut in the center of each of the open walls.

"You can lay out your bed rolls there by the stove," Apsel indicated with a wave of his hand. Reggie and Paul put down their gear.

"I have little food here. We can go to the tavern and get bread and soup. Better yet, we can wash it down with some ale," Apsel suggested. Reggie explained that he and Paul preferred to use their own rations but agreed to accompany him.

It was a ten-minute walk along a well-kept gravel path to the tavern, which consisted of a relatively small one-and-one-half-story stone building, the upper floor of which was, in Reggie's estimation, the tavern keeper's residence. Upon entering, Reggie saw to his right that the tavern had a bar with six simple wooden stools. An unlit barrel-shaped, coal-burning stove stood in the middle of the room. Five small wooden tables surrounded the stove. There was also a table in each of the empty corners to his left. An unlit oil lamp sat in the center of each table. Behind the bar was an open door through which Reggie could see the oven and some of the shelving and utensils of the tavern's kitchen. Unlike Apsel's quarters, this building also had electric lights—a bare-bulbed electric light fixture was attached to the ceiling above each window.

It was just past sunset, and the four naked lightbulbs flooded the tavern with a dull brown light, adding to the warmth of the tavern's dark wood interior. A short, portly, obviously older alien sat on a tall stool behind the bar. Two of the tables were occupied; two men sat together at a table behind the stove, and at the back, left corner table sat a man sleeping with his head cradled in his arms.

Apsel and the two Earthmen chose to sit in the front left corner table where they would have some measure of privacy. After seeing that his two new friends were seated, Apsel went to the bar and shortly thereafter returned with a bowl of thick brown soup and a half loaf of dark bread. Reggie and Paul had each opened a ration pack, which, like the rest of their costume, gear, and accessories, was disguised to look indigenous.

"You are probably better off without this soup," Apsel began as he put down his food and sat down. "The villages now supply little meat. Even the vegetables are poor. I am afraid this is mostly flour and fat.

"I am sorry about the welcome the director gave you," he continued. "But our long habit of being suspicious of strangers is hard to break. We are raised to value secrecy second only to peace."

"We understand." Reggie signaled his acquiescence by spreading his arms open in front of him, elbows slightly bent, palms up. He was beginning to understand the body language. "We will leave tomorrow as soon as we have met with the director."

"I cannot let you leave alone," Apsel responded. "You will never find the way. Wait until the morning after tomorrow, and I will lead you back myself. First I must assemble another trading party."

"Very well. Tell me, Apsel. What exactly is it that your people do here? I saw no fields. What do you eat?"

"Only what we trade for. You have seen our goods. To the farm villages, we trade plant nutrients and insecticides in exchange for food. But we do not just trade for food. To the mining camps, we trade battery-powered electric lights in exchange for coal. To the traders, including the Vikmoor, we provide gas bombs, masks, telescopes, compasses—whatever our scientists can convert into trade goods—in exchange for wire, other electrical equipment, chemicals, and even old books. It is the traders who provide us with the materials necessary to do our research and manufacture our trade goods.

"More I cannot tell you. Maybe the director can. I have said too much already. But I will have another ale before we return to the cabin." He stood up, his wooden chair screeching across the wooden floor as he pushed it back from the table, and made his way to the bar.

Paul spoke softly to Reggie. "It looks like we're not going to have much time to look around, but I'd sure like to get some soil samples."

"Right. And we need to get a look inside some of those buildings. I want to learn as much as we can, but I'm sure that losing Apsel is not going to be easy."

Apsel returned, carrying three mugs of ale. The Earthmen declined the offered beverage. Apsel continued to drink. Rather than let the extra two ales, as he said, "go to waste," he said he would drink those, also. And he continued to talk.

"Usually it is much busier here. This tavern is for traders like us who, when we return from a trade mission, have no fresh food in our pantries. But trade has been so poor that the trading parties are staying out longer. The few who have returned go immediately back out. There is no time to rest." He downed another ale and wiped off his mouth with the back of his arm.

"Trade with the traders is still good," he continued, after wiping his mouth with his arm. "At least we are still getting the chemicals and wire we need. Blaed needs the wire for his electrical division." Apsel downed another half a mug of ale. "He says he needs it to keep the old machines running. Why he bothers, I do not know. He says that his people learn from the very process of making the repairs. And since he does keep such things as the telephone, lights, and even refrigeration equipment working, he may be right. In the meantime, Ophion is keeping his chemical division at work studying the old chemistry texts. The insecticides, nutrients, and gas bombs are by-products of his work."

At this point, the conversation was interrupted by the tavern keeper walking over to, and attempting to awaken, the sleeping loner.

"Get your head up. You cannot sleep here. Does anyone know this man?" A few no's and then silent stares. The tavern keeper jabbed at the loner's shoulder with a long stick and called for him to wake up, with no result.

"I'll have to call the infirmary," he said, mostly to himself, and then disappeared into the backroom.

Apsel took a long gulp and finished most of the last ale. "We better get going. He always sends sleepers and anybody who looks sick to the infirmary—just in case it is The Sickness." The words were somehow capitalized by Apsel's intonation. "And I have had a few too many ales myself. I want to wake up in my own bed at home, not in a bed in the infirmary next to him." He indicated the passed-out loner. They got up, and he led them from the tavern but not before Paul managed to secretly stash a sample of the ale. He dipped a small vial into a half-full mug and unobtrusively held the sample in the palm of his hand until he got outside where he could cap it without anyone noticing.

The two Earthmen steadied Apsel between them as they made their way back to his cabin. Reggie caught Paul's eye as he realized that Apsel's condition would give the astronauts a perfect chance to break away and investigate the city. They could give him a measured application of the scrambler to put him to sleep and then put him to bed. No one would be the wiser. With Apsel safely out of the way, they could have a look around.

It soon became apparent that they were, unfortunately, not going to be left alone. When they arrived at Apsel's cabin, a sentry was waiting outside the front door.

Seeing that Apsel was intoxicated and having trouble walking, the sentry came forward and helped get him into the cabin and onto the bed. Then, as the sentry worked at starting a small fire in the stove, he introduced himself as Krikor and explained that the director had sent him to serve as an "extra guide" in the event Apsel became "indisposed." It seemed that Apsel had a reputation of drinking too much. But the sentry's crossbow, spear, and long knife—weapons that few wore in the city—made it apparent to Reggie that Krikor was more of a guard than a guide.

After lighting the stove, Krikor helped himself to Apsel's meager pantry and began brewing the local equivalent of coffee. He poured a mixture of groundnuts and dried leaves from a ceramic jar into a pot of water and put the pot on top of the stove to boil.

While Krikor was preparing his coffee, Reggie and Paul spread out their bedrolls. Their activity helped mask a set of signals Reggie made to Paul. He caught Paul's eye then raised his touched a finger to his hood, then to his own head and to his scrambler trigger—signaling to Paul to raise his hood because he planned to set off the scrambler.

Krikor was just finishing making the coffee. The pot was at a full boil. After letting it boil for a minute, he poured the contents through a strainer into another pot to settle.

He let it sit while he walked across the room and took three cups from a shelf on the wall to the left of the door leading into the pantry. He offered a cup to both Reggie and Paul, but they declined. Instead, they acted as if they were busy organizing their backpacks. Reggie was waiting for the right opportunity to trigger the scrambler. If Krikor was in the middle of a major sequential activity that required much thought, such as preparing the coffee, he would sense after waking up that something had happened to him.

Now Krikor sat relaxed at the table and began to drink his coffee. "I hear you two probably saved Delmar from losing a leg."

"I don't know, maybe," Reggie responded. Now that Krikor was relaxed and his mind not involved in an activity requiring a chain of complex tasks, he could safely be put to sleep, without the danger of him sensing after he awoke that he had been interrupted. Reggie furtively triggered the scrambler out of burst mode and slowly increased the power. The field spread slowly throughout the room. Krikor soon appeared to become disoriented. He quit talking and looked hazily about the room. Then his eyes blinked several times before closing to mere slits. His next question, asking Reggie and Paul where they were from, ended in midsentence. Then his eyes closed completely, and his head fell slowly to the table.

Moving quickly, the two Earthmen reached into hidden compartments in their packs and pulled out their night-vision goggles. The clear-lensed goggles were not much larger than old-style ski goggles but contained a system of radiation detectors that could selectively scan the natural spectrum from below the visible spectrum through infrared, while laser and radar-type scanners augmented the results. A computer imaging system reproduced the results of the sensor scan onto the inside of the goggle's clear lenses. This allowed the user to see with normal vision contemporaneously with the enhanced image—which was found to improve perception. However, a turn of a control knob could darken the lenses until only the enhanced image could be seen. This was particularly useful when the zoom feature was being used. Another knob controlled brightness. And three separate knobs controlled the goggles' high, low, and midrange spectrum reception, although a fourth was devoted to infrared.

In preparation, Paul pulled his goggles down over his eyes and removed a soil sampling kit from his pack. The sampling kit included two sections of tubing six centimeters in diameter and half a meter long, each. He twisted the two sections together and slung a pouch for samples over his shoulder. Reggie took a stun gun from an inside pouch of his cloak and adjusted it for maximum range for three long-range shots rather than the standard six close-range shots.

CHAPTER 8

Spies

Without speaking, Reggie walked over to the front window and slowly opened one of the two wooden shutters just far enough that he could look outside.

The night-vision goggles' multiple sensor array allowed the astronaut to see very clearly. Instead of being able to see just the gray outlines of buildings that one would normally see at night, the whole image was in clear color. The only thing different from daylight was that there were no extreme shadows—the goggles allowed no hiding places. Reggie reached up with his left hand and turned the goggles' zoom control and searched carefully for sentries. Then he reached up to the right side of the goggles and adjusted the infrared contrast to maximum and searched some more. The high infrared contrast would make anything warmer than the background, including a warm-blooded sentry, stick out like a red beacon on a tower in the desert on a clear night. He saw nothing. "Let's go."

They slid sideways out the door and circled around the house, with Reggie using his infrared goggles to look for life signs. He saw nothing except a few quasi cats and rodents. He could see dim specks of light on the hills but hoped that the sentries that those lights represented were too far away and more concerned with watching for intruders approaching from outside the city than with watching what happened inside the city.

After checking their immediate surroundings, Reggie decided to move on. "Let's just walk right down the sidewalk like we own the place. That way, if anybody does see us, we'll raise less attention. Be ready to take off your goggles. Let's get a contingency soil sample right here,] and then head up toward the manufacturing plant."

Paul unfolded the T handle of the soil sampler and pushed the sampler point down into the ground with his full weight on each handle. The core sampler's counterrotating mechanism drilled and encapsulated a sample of the top fifty centimeters of the soil and then retracted the sample into the upper casing. He ejected the pencil diameter sample into a protective tube and put it in the pouch slung over his shoulder. The entire procedure took less than ten seconds and was accomplished soundlessly. Paul folded the sampler's handle closed, and the two Earthmen headed up the sidewalk toward the manufacturing area.

Not a word was said. After walking the distance of two city blocks, they scanned once more for signs of nearby sentries and then removed their goggles. They knew the goggles would be hard to explain if they were seen. And where they were going, being seen was a very high possibility. With each step they took, distance and time factors alone geometrically increased the odds of the Earthmen being discovered.

They walked in as natural a pace as they knew how. Reggie thought they would be relatively safe until they got beyond the tavern. If caught between it and Apsel's house, he planned to claim they were on their way back for food. But as they passed it, and as its lights faded behind them into the dark, his apprehension increased at every step—he was trained as a test pilot and an astronaut, not as a spy. This kind of work was more for the exoanthropologist.

The only training Reggie had in this kind of work was his survival, escape, and evasion training. But he had not been trained as a spy. He had learned how to live in deserts, swamps, forests, arctic conditions, and even how to survive in alien societies no matter how strange, simple, or complex. He had learned how to live off the land if he had to. He had practiced eating live insects. He had learned how to build lean-tos and snow houses. He had even been taught how to pick locks, hot-wire simple transportation devices, and pick pockets to obtain local currency. But he did not feel ready for this. He knew from what he had been told by Apsel that the villagers prized their solitude and feared discovery by outsiders as a threat to their existence. Reggie briefly wondered if this trip to Poplarville had been rushed. He wondered if they should have first finished at Anaconda so that he could have brought the exoanthropologist.

As they neared the gate into the manufacturing compound, Reggie began to think that they would get away with this late-night excursion without incident and that he was needlessly worrying and second-guessing himself. Success bred new confidence.

They passed through the unguarded gate in the rusting and ancient fence, upon which was posted a much newer-looking sign that translated read simply, "Manufacturing." Grouped together in the front of the compound stood eight identical three-story, redbrick buildings, four to each side of the sidewalk. Each building was twenty meters wide and sixty meters long. They were oriented such that they stretched lengthwise away from the sidewalk, with ten meters separating each from its neighbor. Each stood seven meters back from the sidewalk and was connected to it by a narrower sidewalk that led to the single door in the middle of the front end of each building. All the buildings were dark, except the second one on the right; its ground-floor windows blazed with the harsh white glare of unshielded primitive electric lamps.

At that moment, the building's lights suddenly went dark, and a humanoid shape emerged from the doorway and turned down the walkway toward the two astronauts. With only one streetlamp at each end of this stretch of buildings, the walkway was quite dark. It was too dark to see anything except general shapes. But as the astronauts got closer, Reggie could tell that the alien was probably a worker and not a sentry because he carried no weapons. Yet Reggie was afraid of the consequences if Anton or the guards were nevertheless alerted of their presence. And while it was too late to avoid being seen, Reggie knew that he could not risk stunning the man. That would create a sleeping body that would certainly cause suspicion if found or if the victim was made late for an appointment. There was also the danger that someone might just happen to see it. But Reggie knew that he might have to chance it if the alien gave them any immediate trouble.

Paul turned his head toward Reggie to see what he was going to do. The astronauts exchanged glances, and then Reggie looked straight ahead and kept walking. Paul duplicated Reggie's attempt to look natural. At a distance of three meters, the alien lifted his eyes to the Earthmen, but his attention remained on his self-important everyday routine. He said hello, nodded at the two astronauts, and then simply kept walking, with Reggie and Paul returning his hello as naturally as they could.

The alien briefly wondered why the two strangers, dressed as traders, were in the manufacturing area so late at night. That he had encountered strangers did not seem unusual; there were many people in the city unknown to him. And it was none of his business, he reminded himself. He was not going to act uppity, he said to himself, by intruding into the business of Security. He allowed his mind to again turn to his own problems of his everyday existence.

Reggie thought to himself that it was fortunate that the alien lacked the required aggressiveness and curiosity to pay more attention to them. If the alien was as passive as it appeared, there would be no follow-up reporting or inquiry.

The two astronauts continued along the path, past the building that the worker had just come from, and then turned off into the dark between it and its identical neighbor.

"Paul, get a core sample here. Then I want to take a look inside two or three of these buildings—particularly the one that guy came out of." While Paul prepared the core sampler, Reggie put his night goggles back on and looked around to be certain that there was no one around to see them. As soon as Paul secured the sample, they split up and checked through the window of the two nearest buildings. Reggie went to the farthest one, while Paul looked into the one that the worker had come out of. They both made a video record.

Reggie observed through the windows that the ground floor of his building was divided into several rooms, each of which had several waist-high tables with metal frames on top of them for securing laboratory glassware. Each table had several sinks and apparatus reminiscent of old Bunsen burners. Based on the scale, it looked more like some kind of chemical laboratory than a factory, but Apsel had described this area as the "work area." Above the front door, an old and rusted sign translated as "Prototype Modeling."

Reggie waved the chemist over to him.

Paul quickly glanced inside the building. "Same sort of thing I saw," Paul said. "Basically on the scale of a lab but set up as a small-scale assembly line."

"That's what I thought. Let's look in the next building, too. Then we'll go take a closer look at yours and see what we find."

They moved quickly through the dark around the back of the building and looked through the window of the fourth building down the row. Its ground floor consisted of several large rooms containing lathes, presses, drills, cutters, and other equipment for machining metal.

"We don't have much more time, but I want to see what's upstairs," Reggie said.

Because it was summer and they were in a supposedly secure area, it was not hard to find an unlatched window that was easily pried open. They quickly made their way to a central staircase and up to the second floor. It was divided into large rooms containing small gas ovens and workbenches with more of the Bunsen burners. Racks of glass tubing lined several walls. The equipment appeared to be original, as had that in the machine shop.

"Reggie, I've got a pretty good idea of what this part of the complex was. These buildings made up a research and development area. If we keep looking, we'll probably find an electronics shop. This is all too extensive to have been simply for instruction. These buildings were for serious experimentation and application. A lot of the test gear had to be made to order—that's why they had these shops. It's not that different than what I've seen back on earth. I'd say the first buildings we looked into were designed so that they could be easily configured into various pilot plants. I've seen nothing here laid out like a classroom, so it doesn't look like a school. Plus, there's those old signs that we've seen. I'd say this complex was originally used for research and very small-scale development. Strictly research scale, with breadboard-type setups that these guys are now using for small-scale production."

"Okay, and I've been saving the best for last. I want to see what's so important that that guy was burning the midnight oil."

"Maybe he's just the janitor," Paul half-joked.

"Yeah, maybe, but I want to see."

They quickly made their way back to the darkened building where Paul had started, walking swiftly around and close to the rear of the intervening buildings and running through the dark between them. Reggie was getting more apprehensive. He could think of no rational excuse to give if they were caught in this obviously restricted area.

Looking through the nearest four-paned window, Reggie could see a long row of chemical apparatus and several vats that looked to him like they were for mixing chemicals. Small wooden crates were stacked at one end of the room. He pried open the window, pulled himself up and over the windowsill, and, twisting around, landed feetfirst and immediately made his way toward the nearest row of equipment.

Paul was right behind him, but before he was even over the windowsill, Reggie had found several empty metal casings that were identical to the gas grenades that the innkeeper at the trading post was peddling. Each had a chamber where the chemical ingredients and detonator could be inserted.

As Paul climbed through, he looked briefly at what he surmised was a gas grenade line and came to Reggie's side. Reggie had removed his goggles and begun trying to pry open one of the crates. "These must be the finished grenades," he said. Paul nodded his agreement.

"Paul, see what else you can find while I try to get one of these open. I'd like to get a sample."

Although the lights were out, Paul had little trouble seeing, even without his vision goggles. Both of the planet's moons were full that night and had climbed above the horizon. He soon came to a small room that had a large, fanned ventilating duct that shot up through filters and then through the ceiling. The door was newly marked as what translated as "Quality Control," and Paul guessed that it was used as a gas grenade test chamber. He scraped residue from inside the throat of the air duct and from the walls, floor, and ceiling. He secured the samples in his sample pouch for future analysis and then took more samples from the vats and the apparatus. Further exploration revealed an area apparently used for manufacturing and packaging the insecticides and nutrients that the astronauts had seen the farmers using. By the time Paul was finished, Reggie had grabbed a gas grenade sample.

Stepping outside, they initiated a retrieval beacon in the sample pouch and hid in bushes along the wall, waiting for the arrival signal. When it came, they made a 360-degree sweep for interlopers, sent the all-clear, and threw the pouch into the shadow between the buildings, and the aero droid swooped down for the pickup.

The two Earthmen left as quietly as they had come. They moved quickly through the shadows and down the deserted walkway back through the open mouth of the gates that separated the residential area from the work area. In the bright light of the moons, they could have easily been spotted. They had stayed out longer than they should have. But Reggie had decided that the knowledge to be gained made it a risk work taking. And fortunately, the brisk walk back to Apsel's cabin proved uneventful. Security inside the village was very lax. Strangers were kept out but once in were assumed to belong. Only the more select areas, such as the director's inner sanctum, appeared to have their own guardians.

When the two Earthmen returned to Apsel's cabin, they found that their host and the guard were both still hard asleep. The astronauts quietly slipped into their bedrolls and closed their eyes to rest. Sleep came quickly. It had been a very long day.

CHAPTER 9

The Infirmary

Reggie awoke to the pungent aroma of more of the ersatz "coffee" brewing. Apsel was sitting at the table holding his head up with his hands. He looked a little pale, confirming to Reggie what he had learned on many other planets—hangovers are the same everywhere. Krikor was nowhere to be seen.

"Apsel, you do not look well."

"Keep it down. My head feels even worse than I look. There was a sentry here when I woke up. I guess you met Krikor last night. I sent him to the tavern for bread and cheese. When he returns, we will eat. Then we will go to the infirmary to check on Delmar. They planned to keep him overnight."

Shortly thereafter, Krikor returned.

While Apsel and Krikor ate a satisfying meal of coarse bread and cheese, Reggie and Paul again ate from their own rations. Reggie told Apsel that they could not accept gifts from someone they had helped. "Helping comes from brotherhood, and brotherhood cannot be bought or paid for."

True enough, Reggie thought to himself, but in reality, they were still not sure that the food was safe for them.

Krikor then excused himself, and Apsel led Reggie and Paul to the infirmary to visit Delmar.

"Maybe I can get some medicine for my head and stomach while we are there," Apsel wondered out loud.

They took the same footpath the Earthmen had taken the night before. They passed the building where they had found the gas bombs and could see that during daytime working hours, it was the busiest building of all. They continued along the footpath until they were past the grouping of eight buildings, as well as several others, and then took a side path off to the left. They came to a redbrick and concrete building that was built into the side of the hill. An ancient sign beside the door translated as "Infirmary." Up to their left, they could see the domes and single wall structure they had seen from the opposite hill the day before.

To the infirmary's right, just fifty meters away behind a stand of trees, they could see a squat concrete bunker that looked so solidly embedded into the hill that it seemed to be an outgrowth of the planet's bedrock. It was the size of one small room and had a wall built in front of it as massive as a launch ramp blast wall. It had a single massive door and no windows. Two guards stood at each end of the blast wall, and from the angle where Reggie stood, he could see two more standing in front of the closed door. The building was, in Reggie's estimation, too small to be anything except an entrance to a larger subterranean facility of some kind. Because it was the only building they had seen that was guarded from the outside, he guessed that it must be something considered important; neither the administrative offices nor the gas bomb plant had been guarded. Fortunately, the guards' views of the buildings Reggie and Paul had explored were blocked, and so their explorations had not been detected from there.

They entered the small, two-story, twenty-bed infirmary and were directed by a receptionist/admissions nurse toward Delmar's room. On the way, they passed the drunken man from the night before. He was on his way out. "I guess he checked out okay," Reggie muttered.

Apsel explained that the doctors allowed patients who appeared to be drunk to just sleep it off. If they were not conscious by morning, the doctors knew they were not just drunk. "A simple enough test," Apsel explained, "but sometimes inconvenient for the subject."

Delmar was easily found. He was in good spirits, reported no pain, and said he was to be released that day. The doctor who treated him stopped in to congratulate the two Earthmen on the first aid they had provided. Reggie and Paul's rudimentary, but by Poplarville standards advanced, knowledge of medical techniques bought them a tour of the facility. Reggie welcomed the tour because it would give Paul a good chance to learn about the alien physiology. Because the infirmary was a teaching hospital, it had many educational aids that were extremely valuable. The astronauts were given a newly produced biology textbook and even a slide with a sample of blood that a beginning student had just used to determine his own blood type. It was something unrelated to this that turned out to be even more important.

They were in the back center of the basement level (where the infirmary's pharmacy and laboratory were) when Reggie noticed an elevator that, according to the floor indicators, went only from there to lower levels. Yet the basement was supposedly the hospital's lowest level. This elevator stood next to the elevator that ran between the three floors of the infirmary. The floor level indicator panel above the door on the unexplained elevator indicated that there were three subterranean levels. An X indicator between the basement level of the infirmary and the top subterranean level indicated to Reggie that there was possibly a good deal of distance between those two levels. None of the indicator lights were lit. Neither elevator appeared to be in use. Opposite the elevators stood a closet-sized room that jutted halfway out into the hallway. It had thick-glassed windows and a single steel door. It had what looked like narrow gun ports positioned such that they could lay a covering fire down the length of the hallway. As they walked past, Reggie was able to steal a glance inside, where he saw dark screens that he surmised might have once been video monitors. Apparently it had originally been a guard station. To Reggie, it looked like it guarded the approach to the down elevator, not the way out of it. This indicated that it might have led into a more sensitive area. Since the front door of the infirmary was not similarly guarded, it was reasonable to assume that it was not the infirmary that was the sensitive area. Given Poplarville's obsession with secrecy, finding out where the elevator went would not be easy. Reggie decided to take a gamble.

"I see that the infirmary was originally designed to take casualties directly from the underground areas. It is too bad the elevator no longer works."

"True," the doctor volunteered. "But immediate treatment would not help much with the fatality rate of the cases from down there anyway. I have had men come in several days and even weeks after an accident with gums that have suddenly started bleeding, teeth that are becoming loose, even hair loss. After a time, they usually die. There is nothing I can do in such cases. I can treat the broken bones, concussions, and cuts and bruises from whatever it was that broke or blew apart. But there is little else I can do. Many of our books list remedies for what is called (unintelligible word, not yet translated) sickness, but we have none of the medicines. Whatever it is that they work with down there, it is very dangerous. Of course, because I have no need to know exactly what it is they are doing, I have not been told." Reggie now knew beyond a doubt that something interesting was still taking place in those subterranean levels.

They finished the tour of the infirmary and were led back outside into the late morning sun. They headed toward the main walkway and back the way they had come, but Apsel did take them into one of the manufacturing buildings.

They went into the first building they came to. Like the other manufacturing buildings they had seen, only part of the first floor was laid out for manufacturing. The interior was mostly divided into many rooms with ancient lab tables. Only a section of the first floor had enough space for manufacturing. They could see through open doors that many of the lab rooms were not in use. However, in the open space of the first floor of this building, workers were busy manufacturing telescopes and compasses. "Some of the buildings are not in use," Apsel admitted, "but we use the ones that we need just as our forefathers did. Research is done in the laboratories. Then, what is learned is applied in the factory." He paused for a moment. "Come, it is time for our lunch with the director." Evidently the manufacturing of telescopes and compasses was considered harmless enough for the visitors to see. That was the end of the tour.

Apsel led them back to the administration building. Krikor was leaving as they entered the building. Again, they were escorted into the director's office.

Anton greeted the visitors and led them from his office through a side door into a rectangular room three times as long as his spacious office was wide. A long, highly polished dark wood table ran most of the length of the room. Eight heavy chairs lined each side, and another stood at each end. The size and shape of the table and the layout of the room suggested to Reggie that it was originally intended as a conference room, but a large selection of cheese and bread awaited them at the near end of the table. In the middle of the table, on a small tripod stand, sat a simmering kettle of stew.

The astronauts again declined the alien food, again explaining that it would be contrary to their beliefs to accept gifts in exchange for the help they had provided. Anton did not argue as the two Earthmen began to eat and drink from their packs, although he noted their behavior.

"You two are strange. Someday, I must visit your village. Perhaps we should send our traders there. Did you say it is beyond the long lake?"

"Yes, Director," Reggie answered.

"What do you have to trade?"

"We make pottery, Director, plus whatever goods we have traded pottery for." Pottery was the most innocuous thing they had thought of when composing their cover story. "We've been trading as we go along. We have none of our own goods left to trade, but they are good for storage, canning, that sort of thing."

"Good. I will have Apsel return with you. Perhaps we can use some of your pottery."

"Well, we do not plan on going straight back; we will continue to explore this trade route, even though we have none of our goods remaining."

"Does your village have food?"

"Yes."

"From where?" There was a brief silence. Anton interrupted it himself. "I must be honest with you two. I do not believe you. Krikor very honestly and properly reported to me that he slept last night while he was supposed to be guarding you. Krikor never sleeps on duty, but he could not explain how you could have poisoned him. Besides this of course, you act very strange. You even refuse to eat our food. Perhaps because you poison others, you worry that others may poison you.

"According to our old ways, enemy spies are to be killed, but we are not at war, and it was our own error that brought you here. Perhaps you are innocent. Apsel never should have allowed you to come, but he did, and that was his fault. And you did save Delmar from losing his leg—and maybe saved him from death. But why would you have done these things except to spy on us? I must tell you that I thought of executing you or of not letting you leave, but I will not let our mistake cause your death or loss of freedom. Tomorrow you leave. Apsel tells me he did bring you through a route that was meant to confuse you and make it hard for you to find us again. I will have him see to it that he repeats his precautions on the return journey."

"Thank you, Director. But we helped because, in our village, we are taught that the gods have said that we should treat others as we would have others treat us, not just as others do treat us. There is more to putting others first than acting humble. There is also a practical reason. Agreeing not to do certain things that hurt each other and to support each other is part of the compact we make in living together. We make rules not to steal from others because we care about them and also because we do not want others to steal from us. And we help others not just because we care about them but also because we hope that if we need help they will help us." Reggie decided not to insult this reasonable man with lies. He spoke the truth.

Although he did not tell of their entire mission, he made no direct protest of innocence.

"Whatever brought you here, I would still like to learn of your travels—if any of that part of your story is true. Now, tell me what you have seen. I will decide what to believe."

Reggie started by conveying his impression of the trading village—the decrepit condition, the absence of effective organization, and apparent lack of leadership and initiative. Anton told Reggie that Poplarville's trade records indicated that the same situation was found in many of the villages and that it was getting worse every generation. The harvests in the farming villages where Poplarville obtained its food supplies were constantly getting smaller.

"Our researchers believe it is from the sickness," Anton said. "There are too many deaths. Even Poplarville suffers from it. Some of our scientists work not to advance knowledge but to prove they are better than others. That kind of person eventually gets the sickness and dies. Some call this superstition and coincidence but not me. I admit that I am a religious man and believe there is something to it. Maybe the gods do not cause us to die when we assert our own interests above others; maybe they just meant for the prophets to warn us that if we do act in such a manner that we kill ourselves from the inside. That is what many think today."

They were interrupted by one of Anton's guards, who knocked twice and then entered the dining room through the door from Anton's office. "Excuse the intrusion, Director," he said," but Senior Scientist Blaed is in your office. He insists on seeing you." Anton agreed to see him and turned to his guests.

"Blaed is one of our most prominent scientists. He has done much to teach our people the old knowledge. He teaches what is known of electromagnetism and physics, but I fear that much has been forgotten."

A medium tall and slightly overweight alien soon entered by the same side door that the astronauts had been led through. He filled the doorway from side to side but left considerable headroom. He was sweating profusely, his face was flushed, and he was out of breath. He wore a white, ankle-length lab coat.

"Director," he said, "I must protest the removal of three of my men to Ophion." He got right to the point of his visit. He was as loud as he was plump and direct.

"Very well. What did you have them working on?" Anton asked quietly, in a voice full of both condescension and exasperation.

"I had them rebuilding a wireless communicator. It will be one of my greatest achievements. Ophion will simply use my workers to rebuild some lab equipment."

"That lab equipment is needed by the doctors. They are working on a (the word was garbled by the translator because it was a new word) machine. It will use (next word garbled, identified as a possible form of most recent untranslated word) to photograph bones inside the body. It will aid in identifying broken bones. It will help in treating them."

"Director, this will give Ophion nearly twice as many people as I have."

"I am aware of that." The director spoke in a quiet, even, matter-of-fact tone. "But is the number of people your goal? Use the people you have to increase our trade or help our sick as Ophion has done, and I will give you more people. You have kept the power, lights, and phone lines working, but you have accomplished little of late. It was Ophion who developed the gas bombs and chemicals for the farms. Those are things we can trade. Now he wants to rebuild a machine that will be useful to the doctors. I need results, Blaed. If I leave those three men in your control, who knows what tangent you will send them off on? No, Blaed. The (garbled) machine is to be given priority, but I will reassign the three men to you after the project is finished. After all, you taught them their skills."

"Very well, Director. I will discuss this with you no more. I will return to my work." Blaed showed himself out.

Apsel had been listening quietly to the exchange. "Director, I am afraid Blaed seeks less than knowledge. He is like a child in the playground who refuses to share his toys."

"True. I am afraid our Doctor Blaed may be merely competing with Ophion for workers. Especially now that Ophion is expanding beyond his simple chemistry research. Blaed may feel threatened. He may be making this a battle for resources and control. A turf war. I hate to think that, but I am afraid it is true."

"What about the sickness?"

"Let us both hope that it really is superstition."

The director turned his attention back to his guests. "I am sorry that you had to see such a display. I am saddened by Blaed's actions and what may result. I am going to return to my office. You may finish eating. Then I suggest you prepare for your departure." The director stood to leave.

"Thank you, Director." Reggie stood and bowed his head in acquiescence. "Perhaps someday we may meet again."

Before the director had a chance to leave, there was another knock on the door, which was again followed by one of the guards entering from the director's office. "Excuse me, Director. Dr. Ophion is here and requests to speak with you."

Anton glanced to his guests with an expression of resignation and then told the guard to allow Ophion in, and he and the others again sat down. "At times, I feel like a babysitter. I hope Ophion is not also here to fight about the personnel allocation." The guests sat in awkward silence. Apsel nodded his agreement. The guard escorted Ophion in.

"Greetings, Director. I am sorry to intrude, but I know that Doctor Blaed feels he needs the three men you have assigned to my project. Perhaps he needs them more than I do; I already do have more people than he does, if my technicians and teaching assistants are included."

"Thank you, Dr. Ophion. I am glad you are not here to complain. It is admirable that you are willing to put Dr. Blaed's interests before your own, but results and production must come first. And right now your department is the one giving us results. I will deal with Dr. Blaed."

"Of course, Director. Thank you. I will leave you." The scientist left by the way he had come.

Anton stood up. "Again, gentlemen, I bid you farewell." The director bowed and returned to his office.

"Well," Apsel broke the ensuing silence, "I guess we better start making arrangements to take you back. We must organize a trade party. I fear our previous companions have already departed. We will have to find someone new to join us. Then I will draw our goods and supplies. I would like to leave at dawn tomorrow, but that may be a difficult schedule to meet."

Apsel was correct in his supposition that the schedule was a difficult one. The first problem was finding more men for the trading party. Apsel first led the two Earthmen to the tavern, where, he explained, he always went to find the best prospects. Unfortunately, the only person there this day was the tavern keeper. However, the tavern keeper told tell him that a trading party had just returned and that he expected the whole party to be at the tavern for the evening meal. Apsel decided to return at mealtime.

Apsel's next stop was the warehouse, where he arranged for his trade goods. He reserved two large canisters of dehydrated insecticide and an equal number of canisters of plant nutrients. One box of gas grenades was also reserved, as was a box containing some compasses and a telescope. The astronauts helped load the goods onto back racks so that they would be ready to carry. Then Apsel led them to the commissary where he drew rations for a six-man trading party—including the two Earthmen. He insisted on at least being prepared to feed his two guests, even if they did claim to have their own food. The ration of dried fruits, cereal grains, and corn flour biscuits were packed onto the same kind of back racks that the goods had been.

They returned to the tavern just before dark. Five other traders, all from the single expedition that had returned that day, were already there. All five of them wanted to accompany Apsel on his new trading mission; he had a good reputation for success. Apsel picked the three that appeared to be the strongest and healthiest. Then he bought food, and they all ate together, including the rejected volunteers.

While Apsel huddled with his new partners and made plans, Reggie and Paul turned aside and began discussing what they had seen. Reggie decided that he wanted to investigate the unexplained underground area beneath the infirmary. They would try to slip out as they had the night before.

Apsel's huddle broke up, and the new volunteers left. Apsel told Reggie that he was giving the other men two days to rest and mend their equipment. Everyone was to meet at the tavern and leave from there at dawn in two days. Apsel then suggested that they return to the cabin so that they could start getting their personal gear ready.

On approaching Apsel's cabin, Reggie learned that a second midnight stroll would not be as easy as the first. Outside the cabin, two guards now waited for them, one posted to each side of the door.

The two guards remained outside as Apsel and the two Earthmen settled in. Apsel worked at mending his moccasins while Reggie and Paul sat at the room's single table. "Okay, we'll be here tonight and two more nights," Reggie said quietly to Paul. "Tonight we stay in. I have a plan for tomorrow night, but I need to know if I can drink the ale. Tomorrow we'll get a sample for you to test. Tonight, see what you can learn from the soil samples you took." Paul went to work with his testing equipment, and Reggie joined Apsel.

As Apsel worked at mending his moccasins and other gear, Reggie kept him distracted with conversation. They discussed their planned travel time and whether they would trade anywhere before reaching the trading post. They discussed Apsel's past trips, the successes he had had, and the low expectations he had for this next trip. Apsel's biggest hope was that he would find a new source of food. He intended to trade with independent traders for this information. If there were successful farming villages, the traders would certainly trade that information in exchange for the gas grenades. As Reggie and Apsel talked, Paul sat on the floor on the other side of the room with his back to them. He had his backpack open in front of him and acted like he was arranging its contents and mending clothes. In reality, he was studying the test results of the samples that the aero droid had picked up. He worked for almost half an hour and then went back to the table and sat down. Reggie soon joined him there.

"Nothing interesting in the soil, Lieutenant, but I've got a bonus for you. I've been collecting other samples at every opportunity, and I even managed to get a sample of the ale and food and included them in the sample pouch. The ale is simple fermented grain. Nothing in it to hurt us. The lab's still working on the food samples—they're a bit more complex. What's the plan?"

CHAPTER 10

Quarantined

Reggie was grateful that Paul had shaved an entire day off the timetable. He was worried that their situation could quickly change, and the opportunity to get into the underground areas would be lost. So far, Poplarville was the best lead to the source of the beam weapon. And Reggie had little doubt that if Poplarville did hold the secret to that weapon, it would be in the underground area that the secret could be uncovered.

"Great. Good job," he told Paul. "That means we can go tonight. I need to make an adjustment to your scrambler. Then here's what we'll do." Reggie quickly outlined his plan for getting past the guards posted outside their cabin.

"This'll be a one-man job, but I'll keep in touch with you by radio. If I run into trouble, protect yourself and try to get back to the others."

Reggie called across the room to Apsel. "Apsel, Paul and I would like to thank you for taking care of us by honoring one of your customs. Let's go to the tavern and have some ales. I have some things here we can trade for it. I have some cookware and even some wire. What do you say? We should go tonight, so tomorrow night we can rest."

"I never turn down an offer for ale. Just give me a few minutes to finish this moccasin."

A short time later, the two Earthmen and the alien were seated at one of the tables at the tavern drinking the first of their ales. The two sentries waited outside the door. While Reggie and Paul slowly sipped their drinks, Apsel gulped his down and soon was fairly intoxicated. Taking Apsel's condition as a cue, Reggie knew it was time to put his plan into action. He signaled to Paul, who then raised his hood, triggered his synaptic scrambler at low power, and then slowly increased the power, the scrambler having been set to human.

Having not raised his hood, Reggie soon felt the scrambler's effects. He was lightheaded and slightly disoriented. His senses were dulled, and with dulled auditory nerves, he soon began talking quite loudly. Only his deep training and knowledge of the scrambler's effects allowed him to maintain the control needed to perform his act as a drunken trader. Paul gave a final boost to the power, and Reggie collapsed with his head on the table, just like an unconscious drunkard.

Seeing that he had a sleeper on his hands, the tavern keeper immediately called the infirmary for someone to come and take Reggie away. Apsel tried to use his influence to instead just take Reggie home, but the tavern keeper had a strict policy. As the astronauts had learned earlier, the tavern keeper immediately sent anyone who got sick or passed out to the infirmary, and they were not allowed back until they could prove they were healthy. It was his way of guaranteeing his patrons an epidemic-free establishment. With all of the traders constantly coming back from strange lands, there was always a danger that someone would bring back a new disease. Besides, some of the scientists thought that "the sickness" was like any other disease and could be controlled if isolated and treated.

Two men soon arrived with a stretcher. They took Reggie to the infirmary where a doctor had him laid to rest in a small, single-bed isolation ward.

Apsel and Paul followed them there. Before leaving, Paul leaned low over Reggie's unconscious body and put his ear to his chest. He told Apsel he was checking Reggie's respiration. In reality, he was blocking Apsel's view as he used a spring-loaded injection vile to administer Reggie an electrolytic antidote that would speed recovery from the scrambler. Paul knew the antidote would work quickly, so now he had to get the aliens out just as quickly, while they still thought Reggie was passed out. "He looks okay to me, Apsel. He just can't hold a drink. Let's go home." Apsel agreed that Reggie was obviously just drunk, and so they headed back to his cabin. One of the two sentries followed the doctor down the hallway to the duty station. The sentries had been told by Anton to follow the strangers wherever they went. So one of the sentries would stay at the infirmary, and he figured the night-duty station was as close as he needed to be to either a sleeping drunk or a sleeper. The other sentry followed Paul and Apsel back to the cabin and again posted himself outside the cabin door. Apsel collapsed in bed. Paul lay down and quietly and secretively put a radio receiver in his own ear and waited to hear from Reggie.

With the antidote, it took only a few moments for the scrambler to wear off. As soon as he regained consciousness, Reggie swallowed a stimulant to speed up his recovery. Then he arranged the bedding to make it look like someone was still in the bed. Next, he took off the sole of his boot and took out a tiny transmitter. All of the astronauts' equipment was similarly hidden or disguised. This was done to help them in escape and evasion, as well as to save them from needing to make explanations if their equipment was accidentally discovered. The other heel contained a powerful miniature listening device. Pouches inside the leggings of their boots held a survival knife and light. On this night, Reggie carried his night goggles hidden in a waist pouch inside his tunic. He carried a small set of tools in another pouch. Reggie extended the radio's wire antenna, flipped the switch to transmit, and spoke softly to his partner.

"Okay, Paul. I figure you're not in a situation where you can talk to me, so I'll just tell you I'm okay. I took a stimulant, and I'm fully awake. The light in the room was turned off, so it's pretty dark. There's no sign of the guard or any of the staff or other patients. There is light in the hall, and the light coming through the window in the door to the hallway is giving me plenty of light to see by. I'm looking through that window up and down the hallway, and there's no sign of anybody."

CHAPTER 11

Sabotage

Reggie tried to turn the doorknob, but it moved only a quarter turn. He was locked in. Fortunately, the infirmary had not been built as a prison. A simple trick taught in survival school opened the door easily. Reggie pulled out the blade of his survival knife and slid the blade between the door and the doorframe. He dug the blade into the primitive lock bolt as close to the frame as he could and then made a sideward motion such that the bolt was wiggled free of the frame plate. With his other hand, he simultaneously turned and pulled on the doorknob. He had to work at it a couple of times, but the door finally clicked open. Then he slipped out the door, checked to be certain it could be locked and unlocked from the outside, pulled it closed, locked it behind him, and walked quietly down the hallway in the direction of the elevator.

He could hear voices coming from the duty station at the end of the hallway. He would have to pass that office and then turn right and make his way to a staircase that would lead him to the lower level where the elevator entrance was. Getting closer to the office, he walked on the side of the hallway where the office door was. When within a few feet of the door, he began to inch along sideways, with his back against the wall, listening carefully. Finally he stopped, got down on his hands and knees, and peered into the room from the lower-most corner of the doorway. That was the safest vantage point. He could see that there was a nurse, a doctor, the guard, and two orderlies sitting in the room talking. Reggie could tell from the conversation that the infirmary had at least two other patients—a man with a leg that had been broken and a young boy with a stomach flu. Reggie continued to listen but only watched intermittently. He was waiting for a good opportunity to cross to the other end of the hallway without being seen. He heard someone get up and ask the others if they wanted coffee. He again looked in from down in the corner of the doorway and saw that the doctor had gone over to the coffeepot at the far wall. The doctor had his back to him, and all of the others were looking at the doctor and giving him instructions for their coffee. While they were distracted, Reggie stood up and quickly stepped to the other side of the doorway. He listened for a moment and then began walking quickly but quietly down the hallway toward the staircase that would take him down to the lower level. He was undetected.

The door at the staircase opened easily and revealed a black, unlighted stairwell. Reggie pulled the small pen-sized flashlight from inside his boot and started down the stairs. The door at the bottom of the stairs also opened easily, and he soon stood in the dark hallway next to the elevator shaft.

Reggie could see that the elevator had normally been activated by a card inserted into a slot in a panel next to the door. He hoped that the activator and elevator were still operational. He unfolded a screwdriver from his survival knife, unscrewed four screws from the card mechanism's front plate, and carefully removed the plate. Then he used a blade to short across the electrical connections.

Unfortunately, nothing happened. There did not seem to be any power going through the switch, and he could not get a spark. He quickly disconnected the effected wires at their connection points, stripped them, and twisted them together, in case he could find a way to get the power on. He searched the guard shack for a security switch. He did find a large switch marked "elevator security" and flipped it from "elevator disable" to "enable," but nothing happened. He would have to find another way down, and he had already wasted a full five minutes.

He figured that there must be a backup mechanism that would allow access to the elevator shaft during emergencies. He flashed his light across the face of the elevator doors and located a small hole in the center of the top right-hand door, just fifty centimeters from the top. Reggie guessed that it could be for a key of some kind and searched the guard's office for that key. He used super corrosive to open a locker marked "fireman" and found a long rod with a built-in key in the end. He inserted it the door, twisted until he felt an internal mechanism gently give way, and then by pulling hard to the side, slowly pulled the door open. He pointed his light down the shaft, but it met only darkness. A bundle of cables and wires hung down the center of the shaft. He saw that there was a latch on the inside of the door that would make it easy to open from the inside. He stood on a small ledge and let the spring-loaded elevator door close behind him.

Reggie hung his flashlight by its lanyard around his neck and started what he figured would be a long climb to the bottom. He was right. It took him over fifteen minutes to make the descent. Finally, he could see the top of the elevator car in the distance. Not knowing what may be on the other side, he carefully stepped down onto the elevator car's roof. He looked for and found the car's emergency roof hatch and pried it open with his survival knife. A bright light reflected up through the car, and he was glad he had been quiet. He stuck his head down through the opening, saw nothing, dropped to the floor into a crouch, and concealed himself as best as he could next to the car's front wall. Peering around the opened elevator door, he saw that it opened into a small room that had been a reception area. An empty guard station similar to the one he had seen upstairs sat opposite the elevator door. A large, open steel door led into a hallway. He quickly looked into the guard station and noted that the elevator security switch was in the "disable" position. Then he looked out of the reception room and down the hall. It looked and sounded quiet. To be more certain, Reggie removed a listening device from its hiding place, inserted the earphone in his left ear, and directed the ultrasensitive microphone down the hallway.

The only sounds he could hear were the steady hums of electrical equipment and ventilation equipment and the soft gurgling of fluids through pipelines. He listened carefully for voices or the irregular sounds indicative of humanoid-type activity. He heard none and so continued quietly down the hallway. The hallway had no doors on either side but led to a brightly lit, large, square, white room. Connecting hallways led out from the middle of each wall. The room was one and a half stories high and thirty meters across. In the center of the room, a large cylinder, almost ten meters across, jutted down through the floor and up through the ceiling. A spiral staircase followed the cylinder's outside wall and disappeared through the floor and ceiling. At a landing at floor level, a heavily reinforced steel door blocked the way through the cylinder's wall. A wide array of electronic monitors and controls dotted the walls of the room and cylinder. Based on the number of active and inactive indicator lights and dials, Reggie judged the equipment to be at least partially active. He looked for some kind of monitor or window that would let him see what the cylinder held but could find none. He thought it likely that the cylinder was central to the facility's operation and therefore thought it crucial that he learn more about it. He would have to look inside. And it looked like the only way to do that was by going through that single door in the cylinder's side. He knew there was a certain amount of danger in going through a heavy steel door in what looked like some kind of a laboratory when there was no idea of what was on the other side. He would have liked to investigate further before going in, but he did not have the time. He was concerned that he could be discovered at any moment and might need to escape immediately—before he had time to explore. He needed to budget his time. But something about the heavy steel construction of that door made him hesitate. It sure looked to him like it was intended to keep something contained in the cylinder, but the absence of locks and warning signs finally convinced him it was probably safe.

Reggie turned a wheel in the middle of the door, and its big latches pulled back from the locked position. Being well balanced and oiled, the heavy steel door swung open easily. The exposed cylinder proved to be mostly hollow. He could see that he was on a midlevel of some kind. Stretching straight up and down as far as he could see was a broad tube that reminded him of one of the old terrestrial telescopes, except that it was stationary and was surrounded by a system of hoses, pipes, wires, and coils. At repeating distances, it was encircled by what appeared to Reggie to be massive doughnut-shaped electromagnets. He stepped forward onto a metal grated balcony that circled the inside of the cylinder to get a clearer view of the entire height and depth of the device. Now he could see that a smaller tube ran along next to the main one. Plus, he could see that the cylinder extended so high that it no doubt protruded through the top of the mountain. He went back out, closed the door behind him, and began the long climb to the top of the spiral staircase. An occasional heavy door identical to the first one led inside the cylinder. Presumably these were repair and maintenance access points. At the top of the cylinder, the staircase came to an abrupt end at another one of the heavy steel doors. It, too, opened easily.

He stepped out into the balcony and realized he was standing inside one of the domes they had seen from outside. The balcony had a platform such that it could be swung out to the elbow. The whole setup reminded him of an old-style rocket gantry.

Reggie swung the platform out and stepped across it until he could see that the central tubes terminated in an elbow-shaped collection of coils, tubes, and plates of electromagnets. The elbow was constructed so that it could rotate as well as incline. He guessed that it was a directing mechanism. The second, smaller tube was less heavily constructed and in places was constructed of transparent glass, probably to allow easy observation. Where it ran through the elbow, he could easily distinguish its distinct directing apparatus. It contained heavy-duty, highly reflective mirrors that seemed to be crisscrossed just beneath the surface by coolant lines. Reggie guessed that this smaller tube was meant to direct and focus an intense beam of controlled light energy, possibly to help control the beam produced by the larger tube, but there was no way to tell.

Reggie checked his chronometer. He saw that he had already been gone from his room at the infirmary for almost an hour. He doubted that the infirmary's staff checked on their drunk tank very often. From what he had been told, the normal procedure was to let apparent drunks just sleep off their binges. And he had left the room dark and the door locked, but he had best get moving. The longer he was gone, the greater the chance was that he would be found missing. He decided to go straight to the cylinder's base. He started back down the stairs.

He came to the first control room he had been in but kept going. No other such rooms were encountered until he got to the base. It was a descent of almost fifteen more stories.

The bottom level contained a room very similar to the first one he had been in. But the amount of monitoring equipment this one held made the other room look Spartan. In addition, this room had a large console with multiple monitors and joystick controls, all of which indicated to Reggie that it was the main control room.

Reggie opened the door into the cylinder and saw that it extended one more level below him, and that access was gained by a fiberglass ladder that led down through a hole in the balcony's floor. After climbing down, he saw that at this end of the cylinder, the large tube was connected to a stationary elbow surrounded by coils that led to another tube, which disappeared down a long stretch of horizontal tunnel into the heart of the mountain. But the smaller tube continued straight down and was connected to a vertically hung device that appeared to be an extremely large and powerful laser or similar type device.

To investigate the large tube, he decided to trot a short distance along the tunnel into the mountain and was soon glad he did. In a little less than a minute, he came to a section of the tunnel with a ceiling two stories high. A ladder led up to what looked like an observation platform, with a window that faced out toward the direction of the continuing tunnel. He climbed up the ladder, looked through the window, and saw that he was looking out into what looked like a very expansive room—he could not even see the walls and ceiling—partially because it was very dimly lit. He put on his night-vision goggles and saw that he was looking not into a large room but into a wide, flat valley—no doubt over a mile across. He looked out across the valley and thought there was something strange looking about the vegetation. The valley floor looked like the floor of a forest but without the trees, just stunted undergrowth. None of this topography looked anything at all like the recognizance photos he had seen. He adjusted the zoom on his goggles and saw that a large, circular ring-shaped mound stretched from the near side of the valley all the way to the far side—a full mile in diameter. He could see that the tunnel he was in continued on inside a dirt-covered mound as it left the mountain and intersected the ring at an oblique angle.

Reggie instinctively looked up and tried to see one of the moons so that he could check his bearings, but there was no moon. It looked like there was some kind of obstruction between him and the sky. There were places where he could see long expanses of stars or blotches of stars, but the darkness was too complete and the edges of visible sky were too abrupt to be accounted for by clouds. He adjusted the zoom, sensitivity, and focus of his goggles, and the answer soon became clear. A system of cables held some kind of canopy netting suspended over the valley floor. It was a very effective although not very sophisticated job of camouflaging. The optical images had missed it, and the other imaging systems were being used to search the floor of the oceans and seas for impact craters. It was even possible that the cables held antennas and transmitters designed to interfere with sensors. The canopy was just enough to hold the camouflage. Some light still got through. That explained why the valley had only stunted and shade-favoring vegetation.

Reggie knew that the buried ring had to contain some sort of particle accelerator. There was no doubt in his mind that he had discovered the particle beam device that was taking potshots at the *Cutty*'s probes, or at least one of a battery of such weapons. It was probably this kind of machine that had knocked out the electronic components of the lander. With the planet's low magnetic field and the high energies this huge system could generate, it would constitute a formidable weapon. He also knew that lasers could be used effectively to help control a particle beam's trajectory. The laser attached to the beam system's side was probably there for that very reason. The *Cutty*'s crew probably had not seen it because the lander, as well as the probes, had all landed in bright sunlight. And that big screen he had seen was no doubt an antenna. An antenna can receive but also transmit. Hard telling what all they were experimenting with here and then putting into practice. But to Reggie, it all seemed to add up to a weapon system.

Fearing he was running out of luck and time, Reggie ran all the way back to the lower control station. He quickly took a set of pictures and then took a moment to study what appeared to be the main control console. It was divided into three equal sections. The side sections sat at a forty-five-degree angle to the center section, such that they were all within easy reach of a single central chair. The console faced a large map of the continent that was marked with a system of five small triangular markers. Four of them were evenly dispersed on the continent's outer frontier, and the fifth was inside the perimeter but very much off center and not part of any discernible pattern. The markers were all dark except two, which were lit green. One was the one that was the farthest to the west. The other seemed to mark his current location in the center. The center section of the console was subdivided into five subpanels. Each panel had a vertical row of controls and lights. Two columns were active and had a green light shining at the top of the column. Below that, each had a switch and lights with a label that translated to "auto/manual." These were turned to "auto." Below that were illuminated switches labeled "fail-safe on/off," a small monitor screen labeled "targeting," two illuminated button switches labeled "targeting/radiate," a three-position switch labeled "off/standby/ready," and at the bottom, a joystick with a red button at the top of its hand grip. The fail-safe switches were switched to "on," and the three position switches were turned to "standby."

Reggie turned the fail-safe switches to "off," and the green triangles on the map turned to yellow, and the panels turned dark. However, he discovered that if the fail-safe switch was turned to "on" and the "off/standby/ready" switch was turned to "off," the green triangle on the map remained on, but an accompanying red light also came on. He turned the switches back to their original positions of "on" and "standby," and the red light went off, and the green light at the top of the column showed green.

The right-section console contained a computer terminal. At the top were five one-inch-square button switches labeled "computer engage." Each switch was depressed, and two were lit internally with green lights. A series of inactive indicators and diagnostic lights indicated that only these computers were functioning. The left-section console contained a communications terminal. It also was divided into five sections. Two sections had two glowing green lights, one labeled "network" and the other "internal."

Reggie stepped up to the large map that the console faced and found that it swung open on large hinges. He swung it open and saw that the wiring arrangement was very simple. Behind each triangle, sets of wires led to a green light and a yellow light. Reggie decided to get to work. He closed the map and went back to the main console.

He stood facing the center console. Each of the five subpanels had small handles at the top and bottom that were obviously intended as grips for pulling the subpanels out of the main console. He turned all of the switches to "off" on one of the subpanels that was topped by a green light. Then he twisted the two toggle nuts located at the panel's top and bottom and pulled gently but firmly straight out on the handles, and the panel's module slid smoothly out like a well-oiled drawer. With the back of the switches now exposed, Reggie had little difficulty replacing a small section of the wire leading to the "fail-safe" switch with a piece of slow electrolytic decomposing wire from the sabotage equipment in his escape and evasion kit. He did the same thing to the "auto/manual" switch. Once turned on, the electric current would cause the wire to slowly decompose. He figured it would take at least several days, and by that time he and Paul would be long gone. Meanwhile, if the equipment were tested, it would work perfectly normally. He reinstalled the panel, turned the switches back on, and repeated the operation on the other lit panel.

Time was running short, but Reggie ran up the stairs back to the dome to further disable the beam system. He now preferred the risk of getting caught, which he felt he had some control over, to the unknown risk of some backup system taking over for the sabotaged controls.

He was out of breath and his heart was pounding by the time he got back to the dome. Not waiting to rest, he swung the gantry out to the beam's directional system. He wanted another way to disable the weapon that would not be readily noticeable. With but a moment's hesitation, he reached out to one of the power lead connections that fed an electric motor that controlled one of the directional magnets. He pulled the connector out, broke off one of its prongs, and pushed the prong and connector back into place, the circuit broken. Not very sophisticated, he thought to himself, but given the miles of wire that ran through this system, it would take awhile to find. The natural tendency in checking the connection would be to just push it home to be sure it was tight, not pull it out to look at it. Next, he gave a few turns to a crank that controlled one of the focusing magnets. He hoped that would put the system's calibration out of focus. Then he swung the gantry back to its storage position. For good measure, he decided to disable the dome mechanism. That way, even if someone did test the weapon and got it working, they still would not be able to open the dome to use it. To allow a clear zone of fire, the entire dome could be rotated 360 degrees. It was powered by four electric motors. Reggie shimmied up a conduit and onto a ledge that ran around the inside of the base of the dome. From there, he squeezed along the ledge and reversed the wires on two of the four motors. Running in reverse to the others, this would make the dome difficult to maneuver, yet it could be awhile before the problem was recognized as anything other than sloppy maintenance.

It was not a real professional sabotage job, but Reggie doubted his work would be noticed before he and Paul left the village. If it was noticed, Anton would probably guess they had something to do with it and either detain or execute them. Anything was possible. Reggie hoped that the sabotage would not be discovered until after someone actually tried to fire the beam. By that time, it would be too late to fire it; the lander would be well on its way to orbit.

Reggie suspected that the system was automated. He doubted that the villagers had any idea of how to analyze and repair its malfunctions, or even how the controls worked. He figured that the trigger controls were just a backup system. The aliens just did not seem to have the sophistication necessary to do anything other than routine maintenance. That the equipment still worked was more of a testament to Poplarville's ancestors than it was a measure of current capabilities. So even if the aliens did find out that something was wrong, he doubted they could fix it.

Time was now of the essence. Reggie raced down the stairs to the middle control room, ran up the hall to the lower guard station, hoped for the best, switched the security switch to "enable," and raced toward the elevator door. With both switches now on enable, he was rewarded with the sight of the elevator lights coming on and the doors beginning to slide closed. He squeezed through sideways just as the doors shut. He hit the button for the top level, and the elevator rushed up toward the infirmary. Less than a minute later, the elevator stopped, and the doors slid open—exposing the dark corridor. Light flooded from the open elevator into the dark hallway. Reggie punched the button that would send the elevator back down and stepped out of the elevator. Then he disconnected the hot wire he had rigged in the card box and put the box back together the way he had found it.

The mission had gone well. Fortunately, the facility had been built for a level of security more typical of academia than of the military or industry. He could not believe how easy it was to get the elevator door opened. The facility may have been built so as to be sheltered, but it was not built as a fortress. It was possible that the underground portion of the facility was put there to take advantage of tunnels built to connect the research labs to the valley where the accelerator had to be built. A large area of flat ground, such as that in the camouflaged valley, had been required for the accelerator. The materials and construction techniques used in most of the surface buildings appeared to predate the underground areas. It looked as if the military may have preempted a facility that was originally meant for research. If the beam system had been built there for the purpose of defending the village, there would probably be evidence of better security systems. The facility just did not appear to be that well guarded. Reggie thought it more likely that the scientists had built a prototype, and the design had been put into production but with the prototype hooked into a battery of beam weapons so as to augment the system's interior firepower. Reggie could not help but feel that the low grade of the security provisions proved it was primarily constructed and controlled by academic minds, not military ones.

Reggie made his way back up the stairs and down the hall, and again slipped passed the doctor's duty station. He made his way quietly back to his room. The fact that it was undisturbed indicated that his absence had not been discovered. He locked the door, reported to Paul by radio what had happened, returned his gear to its hiding place, lay down, and fell fast asleep. He was unaware that just a few minutes later, the nurse made his rounds, looked through the door window, saw that Reggie was asleep, checked the door, and slowly continued his routine rounds.

CHAPTER 12

Answers

It was not the bright sun of the beginning of another day that coaxed Reggie awake, although the hot white sun blazed brightly through a light fog that morning. Having no windows, Reggie's room remained dark, and the astronaut continued to sleep. Rather, he was startled awake by the metallic click of the unlocking of the door. He blinked his eyes several times, forced them to focus, sat up, turned, and swung his feet to the floor as the doctor, a nurse and an orderly entered and switched on the light. Reggie sat with his face in his hands and his elbows on his knees. He did not want to appear to be anything other than hungover. The medical staff was quite familiar with the tavern keeper's habit of sending people to the infirmary who were nothing more than drunk. Neither drunks nor the waste of time they created were highly thought of. For that reason, no one bothered to give Reggie a physical. Just as they did with all the drunks, the staff simply let him sleep it off and then shoved him out. The fact that the patient awoke was considered test enough. Because this was the regular test, no one had even bothered to investigate his condition when he had been brought in. After all, if he did have some kind of plague, there was no point in getting too close to him. This was a chance Reggie had taken, for if anyone had checked even his temperature and pulse, he would have had a serious problem, because both were highly out of the alien anatomy's norms. The astronaut's external appearance had been disguised but not his internal appearance.

The sun was well above the horizon as Reggie stepped out of the infirmary into the lifting morning fog. His guard was dutifully waiting. Together, they headed back to Apsel's cabin.

The morning fog was also lifting at the agricultural village of Anaconda. Mark gazed out a second-floor window of the trading post as he and Judy finished their breakfast of cold, disguised survival rations. The two astronauts had settled into a quiet routine of gathering samples and testing them in their field labs. They combined the disciplines of anthropology and archaeology. From interviews and archaeological evidence, they concluded that the village was originally the site of a single farmhouse. They had located its abandoned foundation. The hospitality of its owners, the good farming conditions, and the farm's prime location at the intersection of two navigable streams had led others to settle there, also. The growing community had worked together to build the trading post, hoping it would entice others to come there to trade. Mark could not determine, however, why the village was now so completely disorganized and devoid of direction and leadership. He had heard about the "sleeping sickness," but that did not explain the village's deterioration. The inhabitants were so determined to put others before themselves that no one would step forward to be a leader of any kind. This was the part that Mark had not figured out. It seemed to be a new or perhaps newly reinforced attribute of the culture's values. Obviously, the villagers had at one time been organized enough to lay out and construct the trading post. But now the village was totally devoid of leadership and direction. Furthermore, the villagers were individually totally without initiative.

The villagers' relationship with the Vikmoor was another thing Mark could not understand. On his and Judy's second day at the village, they had had their first encounter with them. A band of ten Vikmoor had arrived at the village, demanded and received all the ale they could drink, and then had their sacks filled with grain. The villagers received nothing in return and did not resist. They instead went out of their way to give into and even assist the Vikmoor. When one of the Vikmoor's bags full of grain stolen from the villagers broke at the seams, one of the villagers offered to replace it. Mark had seen defeated people before. He had even studied and personally interviewed victims affected by the Stockholm syndrome. Here, though, there was something entirely different going on. The villagers did not identify or sympathize with the Vikmoor. Perhaps the villagers simply acted out of fear, but the one who had offered to replace the broken grain bag had actually looked disappointed when her offer was refused. Mark wondered why the villagers acted that way. He saw that they had started to enclose the village with a wooden stockade, but the project sat unfinished. After the Vikmoor left, Mark confronted the innkeeper as to why no one resisted. The answer puzzled him.

"Our fathers and grandfathers resisted, sometimes successfully. For a time, we stopped them, but to resist is not the way to peace. Even though we could have defeated them, our selfishness and anger burned within, and many of us died from the sickness. We had forgotten true freedom and the true way to peace.

"People are to be valued above material possessions. Violence resolves few things. The gods weeded out those who did not understand that. Resistance does not change the needs of others. If someone needs something, I should share what I have—whether I am politely asked or rudely asked. It is easy to be gracious to friends and beggars, harder to help those who are not grateful. But the truly helpful will help all men and thereby prove their own goodness. Constantly desiring, hoarding, and not sharing possessions leads to conflict and war. Others should always be put first. Allowing myself to get angry and violate the ideals of peace makes me a slave to that which provokes me. It changes me. My provoker has changed me and my peaceful state of mind. In succeeding in changing me, he has already beaten me. He has enslaved me. It is only by not changing that I can win.

"If your enemy strikes you, turn your cheek that he may strike the other also, and in so doing, prove you are free. Striking back does not resolve the underlying problem. Violence solves nothing."

"You sound more like a philosopher, or maybe a priest, than you do a tavern keeper."

"Oh, I guess a tavern keeper gets to hear more philosophizing than most. We sure hear a lot of confessions and learn about a lot of personal problems."

Mark was not sure if this philosophy was a rationalization for the way the people were beaten down or whether it really was a nonviolent and self-denying culture. The philosophy he had heard them speak sounded all right to him on the surface. The people truly seemed to live it. They followed it in their relationships among themselves as well as with outsiders. He saw no competition, only subservience, but he still did not understand the absence of initiative and drive.

Reggie and Paul spent that day with Apsel as he prepared for their departure. Apsel worked all morning, mending his clothes and gear, and then washed what was dirty in a tin basin and hung it up to dry on a rope along one of the cabin's inside walls. Reggie washed and mended some of his own clothes before engaging Apsel in light conversation about hunting wild game, but it seemed Apsel had little experience or knowledge of hunting. With Apsel distracted, Paul worked discreetly analyzing some of the samples they had taken.

Most of Paul's work was done automatically by the computers in his test kits. All he had to do was prepare and insert the samples. However, there were limits to his field equipment. He decided to ask Reggie for help in uploading some of the data to the *Cutty Sark* for analysis. Reggie was in the middle of a discussion with Apsel over the merits of pure exploration.

"We never explore just to see what is there," Apsel was saying. "We only go where we think there may be opportunities to trade."

"But your scientists work for the advancement of knowledge, regardless of the returns. Why not the same for explorers?" Reggie argued.

"That is only partially true. You heard the administrator telling Blaed he must get results from his work. Although Ophion works partly for knowledge, he is fortunate that others have recognized the trade applications of his discoveries.

"Those who do the best research and learning usually manage to rise to the top of their departments. They receive the most resources for future work based on what they have accomplished in the past. Most are too happy and involved in their work to notice what anyone else is doing. Most do not care who is called boss, so they blindly go about their studies. Fortunately, some among us are more practical minded, and the practical applications of the research are eventually put to use.

"It is up to us traders to supply the village and the scientists with the things needed to live and continue the research. Of course, without the things the scientists have developed for trade, we could not do our trading. We are necessary to each other. If traders go out and come back empty-handed, as would happen if we went out just to explore, the entire village, including relearning, research, education, and the application of those things—that is, production—would all suffer. If we have less production, we have less to trade with."

"Excuse me. Reggie?" Paul tried to politely break into the conversation. Reggie and the alien looked over to him. "Could I see you for a minute?"

"Yeah, sure." Reggie began getting up from the floor, where he had been sitting cross-legged across from Apsel while the alien was restocking his fire-starter kit. "Excuse me, Apsel." The alien waved the Earthman off with a friendly wave and bent down to concentrate more fully on his work.

Reggie crossed the room and sat down on the floor next to Paul, who began to speak quietly so that Apsel could not hear.

"Reggie, I'd like to upload this data to the *Cutty* so that we can get a better analysis. She should be just coming over the horizon. I can do it without Apsel seeing me if you sit here and act like we're talking for a minute."

To Apsel, it looked like his two visitors were having an important conversation. In reality, Paul had contacted his ship and uploaded his data to the chemistry department's analyzers. As soon as he had made the contact and uploaded the data, no more verbal contact would be necessary from his end. Paul nodded to Reggie, who then got up and went back to sit with Apsel. Reggie told Apsel that they were discussing their need to be continuing with their own exploration. Then he changed the subject, and the two men began to discuss the weather conditions and what things Apsel normally did for entertainment. Paul continued to look busy with his own pack and gear. After just a few minutes, he had put everything away and was laying on his bedroll—seemingly resting. In reality, he was waiting for the *Cutty*'s next orbit, when it would transmit the results of the analysis work back down to him.

It was late morning when Apsel had completed most of his personal preparations, so he offered to take the two Earthmen on a further tour of the village. He was not accustomed to spending so much time inside and said that he needed the break. He even took them into the gas grenade plant. Again, for all of the villagers' concerns about secrecy, it was keeping things secret from the outside world that appeared to be the issue, and Reggie and Paul had become exceptions. To Reggie, this was another indication that the facility's original inhabitants were not of a military culture. Any military culture he had ever seen had handled classified information on a need-to-know basis. He did not see how Poplarville's inhabitants could have retained the overall aspect of secrecy and yet lose that important application if its principles.

Apsel had an ulterior motive for going to the gas grenade plant. He had an old friend who worked there, and he wanted to see if there was anything new that could be obtained for trading.

While Apsel and his friend talked, the two astronauts wandered off and unobtrusively looked around. Not much had changed since their clandestine visit, but it was obvious that more grenades had been produced and crated.

Having a few moments to themselves, Paul reported to Reggie what he had learned from the *Cutty*'s tests. He told him that the tests had detected the same toxic thioether derivative in the samples from the gas bomb test chamber as had been found at the residential area of the chemical plant.

"It's compounded from carbon, hydrogen, sulfur, and chlorine. That's sure consistent with what's in this lab. It's actually a liquid, and it's an extremely powerful vesicant—that is, blistering agent. And I learned from a cross-check of the *Cutty*'s library that an identical substance was used as a weapon on early twentieth-century Earth.

"Back then it was called mustard gas," Paul explained. "Gas masks were soon developed as a defense, so the gas had limited strategic success. If a soldier was caught in a gas attack unprepared, however, the blistering could cause blindness, permanent respiratory problems, or an agonizing death. The weapon was considered to be so cruel that it was eventually outlawed by international agreement. That ban came from a society that tolerated the indiscriminate bombing of civilian populations by massive air attacks and rocket bombardment. That tells you how bad this mustard gas really was."

"And it seems that the gas bombs made here were used in attacks on the chemical plant?"

"I'd say so. I transmitted data from samples taken from both the bomb factory and from the chemical plant up to the *Cutty*, and they were nearly identical. And we haven't heard about any other people around here with a technology sophisticated enough to make them."

"Was it used at Anaconda?"

"No, no sign of it there. As a matter of fact, I went back and checked all of my soil samples and found no other evidence of it at all. I even had the *Cutty* scan the planet from orbit. There's only localized evidence of it. There's no evidence that it was used on a planetary, or even continental, scale."

"So it was probably not the source of the planet's problems?"

"Probably not. But if it was used today against anyone who was unprepared or incapable of defending against it, the effects would be devastating."

Apsel finished talking to his friend and turned toward the Earthmen, who ended their discussion.

"Well, there is nothing new here," Apsel told them. "Let us make one more stop while we are here. I want to take you across the street to the bio lab. It is where our few medical scientists are studying the sleeping sickness. My cousin works there. What they are doing is very interesting."

Apsel led the astronauts into another one of the eight identical redbrick buildings that comprised the active section of the research and manufacturing area. He took them into one of the ground-floor laboratories, where several men and women, all in long white lab coats, were bent over microscopes, glass laboratory equipment, small centrifuges, and Bunsen burners. The scientists glanced briefly at the three visitors, and then all but one of them went back to their work. The one who allowed the interruption to continue straightened up from a microscope, stretched, and then, arms outstretched, smiled broadly as he walked across the room to welcome the approaching Apsel.

"Apsel, my cousin, how glad I am to see you. These must be the visitors I have heard so much about." The news of the visitors was obviously traveling fast.

"Yes, Alo, these are the ones who saved the life of one of my men. I am going to be leading them back to Anaconda soon, and we are taking a break from our preparations. So far they have learned nothing from us except religion. I wanted them to see what you are doing here. They are from far away, so I thought you may like to meet them."

"True, very true." Alo greeted each Earthman with outstretched, open arms. "But we are not trying to replace religion, Apsel. We are trying to learn how the gods work and so get to know them better. That is the purpose of science, is it not?"

"Yes, Alo, so you have told us, and so have Blaed and Ophion. But show us what you are learning here."

"It is really interesting, I hope you will admit. We have here frozen samples taken from every Poplarville citizen who has died since the war. We have four generations of tissue samples and even some whole bodies stored in our freezers.

"Our records show that our great-great-grandfathers knew that there was a common disease that was ravaging the population. Come with me." He led them to a staircase and then into the basement as he continued to talk. "They knew that they had to keep very good data and samples if they were to learn what was happening." They continued to walk and entered a large room.

"An interesting aspect is the demographics of this disease. At first it struck the old as much as the young." He pulled open a long, deep drawer, and the air turning to frost above it showed it to be a deep freeze. It contained an object shaped like a man covered by a blanket. Alo pulled back the blanket as far as the upper chest. It was the frozen body of one of the aliens. Its face was covered with frozen open sores. Alo slid the cabinet closed. "Those who died looking like this died of something they could not identify. It struck both the young and the old. Surely you have seen this before. It became known as the sleeping sickness.

"Anyway, what we have found is that over time, older people have not as often died from this." He slid open another cabinet. It contained a young child, probably two years old or less by earth standards. It was covered with the same frozen sores. "Peculiar. It seems that not only are fewer dying from the disease today, but very few older people die from it." He led them back upstairs and into an office. A graph chart hung prominently on one wall. "See, this line represents the village's total population over the past four generations." His right index finger stabbed the chart. "This one traces the total deaths." He continued to indicate which line he was discussing. "This one shows the number of deaths caused by the disease, as determined by the open sores. This one traces those who died from it who were over the age of forty. This one traces those who were between forty and twenty, this one ten to twenty, this one ten to three, one to three, and less. In the first generation, it struck all age groups equally. But in the second generation, it struck mostly the young. See? The ones dying at older ages declined every year. The rate for those dying at a young age declined more slowly. Many still die from it, but it looks as if the disease is decreasing, whatever it is. And look at this." He turned to an electron microscope. "We have found this virus in everyone who died from the disease."

"See?" Apsel began. "My brother claims it is a disease that has been killing us, not the wrath of the gods."

"I have told you Apsel," Alo replied, "I do not believe in coincidence. The virus must be connected to the deaths. The gods work in mysterious ways. By learning their ways, I will get to know them."

"I do not believe the gods would wipe out the innocent young," Apsel argued. "If they died from this disease of yours, it cannot have anything to do with the gods. And it does not explain the Vikmoor."

"Excuse me, Alo," Paul interrupted, "but have you taken any broad-based samples of the general Poplarville population?"

"Yes, that's a good point," Alo replied. "We took samples from both the general Poplarville population and our own. We found that nearly everyone carries the virus almost from birth. Nearly every adult is a carrier. It seems to lay dormant until something triggers it. It is found in the old as well as the young.

"We have also studied those who have had bursts of aggressiveness or anger, taking several samples over a number of days. This was done in conjunction with interviews of the subjects and their families and acquaintances. In all of them in which the targeted mental condition was long lasting or particularly intense, we have seen an almost immediate multiplication of the virus—and the host soon died. Sometimes it first manifests itself with the unconsciousness that gave it its name. But in cases of very intense emotions, the sores appear within the first six to twelve hours. And in those cases, death comes more quickly.

"The fact that there are now fewer victims tells us that an immunity is evolving. Or perhaps there are fewer subjects in the population with the targeted aggressive type behavior. This latter view is supported by interviews of the general population. We have found no instance of aggressiveness that was not accompanied by an onslaught of the disease."

"What about environmental factors?" Paul asked.

"We have found nothing in the diet or environment of those who get the disease that is different from those who do not, so we conclude that it is a difference in behavior."

"I still do not understand how it could be that if we all carry the disease, we do not all die from it," said Apsel.

"It may be a miracle of faith that allows us to live more peacefully today. Perhaps the gods are using the disease to kill those of us who harbor hateful thoughts. The gods, angered by the Great War, decided to sever that unhealthy vine among us, at the roots. Now, only the peaceful remain to bear fruit," concluded Alo.

"But enough of this," the alien scientist said, terminating their discussion of the sickness. "Tell me about your adventures," he said to Reggie.

And so, the four of them sat in Alo's office, and the astronauts told Alo what they had seen—the poisoned lake, the backward agricultural village, and the deserted chemical plant. Then, Apsel and Alo sat and drank coffee while the four of them made small talk about the preparations for the expedition.

After leaving Alo's laboratory, the three men went back to Apsel's cabin. Apsel took some time to manufacture some fishing lures and then announced he was ready for the expedition. "Let's rest and then go over to the tavern for an early supper and a few ales." But their plans were soon changed when one of Anton's assistants appeared with an invitation for them to dinner.

The food at Anton's was again plentiful, but again, Reggie and Paul ate their own rations, and once again the administrator made it clear that he did not believe Reggie's story of who he and Paul were and why they were there. Reggie knew he did not have a sufficient cover story prepared about the village he and Paul were supposedly from, so he tried to concentrate on descriptions of what he had actually seen.

"One thing I should let you know about is the abandoned chemical plant we discovered. It is just a short distance downriver from Anaconda. It looks like there was a thriving village there for a while, until recently, when it was apparently attacked by someone using your gas bombs. It looks like your bombs destroyed the village."

"Interesting."

"Did you know your bombs were being used to attack villages?"

"That is really none of our concern. We trade for materials that can be used to make nutrients and insecticide, and for materials that we need for instruction and experimentation in our laboratories. We also trade for food. This trade is what keeps this city, this center of learning and relearning, alive and strong. We have no control over how the things we trade away are used. The insecticides and nutrients we develop, and the learning and relearning we do here, are all for the common good, the betterment of everyone, not just for our own welfare."

Reggie decided it was not productive to argue with the administrator. Instead, he continued his narrative and described the lake in which the lander had crashed. He described how it was so full with toxic chemicals that its normal biosphere had been destroyed.

The administrator agreed that the destruction was probably caused by chemicals discharged from deteriorating chemical plants and storage facilities. He also agreed that the contamination was not the cause of his civilization's downfall. Rather, he said that a war had started that had ended in catastrophe. Explosions "high in the sky" had destroyed all electrical equipment. Then, as if that was not enough, people began to die from a deadly plague. Priests attributed the disease to the gods' wrath, "sent to destroy those who had not learned that it is the meek who inherit peace and happiness, not those who put themselves before others."

"I am not sure that I have total faith in what the priests teach, but I do believe that it is best to work with others rather than against them," the administrator continued. "I prefer to think I am a man of science, not superstition. I believe in self-fulfilling prophecy, fear, and coincidence, not in things I cannot see."

They finished the meal in awkward silence. Then Apsel took the two astronauts back to his cabin. He said that he had a meeting to go to in which he would be given the compiled reports of all the traders who had recently returned. He would be given up-to-date information on trade prospects and would receive instructions on what to trade for. Because of the trade information that would be discussed, he asked the Earthmen to wait for him at the cabin. "I guess he appreciates the necessity of mercantile confidentiality," Reggie remarked to Paul.

Paul used their seclusion to test more samples. The "guide" that had been assigned to them in Apsel's absence was standing sentry outside and so was not a threat. Paul had yet to find anything poisonous to themselves or the aliens, except the gas bombs and the chemicals in the lake and at the chemical plant. He ran more checks on his old samples as well as preliminary tests on samples he had just obtained. Reggie used the opportunity to call the *Cutty Sark*. Connors was on the bridge when Reggie called. They discussed Reggie's mission of the previous night, and then Connors told him that Jake was ready to fly the lander up onto the beach to make the final repairs.

"Well, Captain, it looks like we're making progress. At least now we're back to where we started—figuring out what killed this place. I'm sure Jake and Eric will have us ready to go to orbit in no time, and I'm pretty confident that we'll find out what happened to this planet. Apparently, there was some kind of a plague that hit here. At least we've heard a lot of stories about the mass deaths of anybody who didn't measure up to the culture's standards of passivity. A lot of myths have a factual foundation, so we'll try to follow up on this angle.

"Tomorrow we're heading back to the other village. If Elizabeth hasn't uncovered any good clues, we'll move closer to one of the old cities and see if we can find any mass graves to exhume. They ought to tell us something. And we've got the slide we were given. I'll try to get those to Elizabeth."

Reggie signed off and made final preparations to leave. Apsel soon returned, and the three of them bedded down for the night.

CHAPTER 13

Prisoners

Long before dawn, Apsel woke the two Earthmen. It was time to begin the long walk back to the agricultural village. After dressing and packing their few personal items, they went to the tavern and met up with the three new team members. They had a breakfast of hard rolls and coffee (the Earthmen now knowing they could safely eat the alien food) and were on their way as the sun cleared the horizon.

At the agricultural village, Judy and Mark were continuing their routine of investigation and analysis. They were working in the village cemetery, which was out of sight of the village, off the trail leading to the north. Judy had recorded the date of death and other data contained on the tombstones of the marked graves and was at that time using an inconspicuous miniature radar scanner to search for unmarked graves. The evidence indicated that there had been many more deaths in the town's early history but that the deaths had steadily become less frequent over time. They had worked in the village dump the day before. Based on refuse patterns, the village had undergone an initial period of material scarcity, then sufficiency, and now scarcity again. This conclusion was based on the abundance and quality of discarded items, including such evidence as discarded food matter. In times of scarcity, less was discarded, and the qualities of the manufactured goods—evidenced by the quality of such things as pieces of broken, discarded pottery—were clearly inferior. Based on these patterns and the general dilapidated condition of the village, Judy believed that it had been in a general decline for the past several years. They had also searched the dump for signs of organic and inorganic contaminants. Now, at the isolated cemetery, Judy was using a long drill-probe to obtain biopsies from a wide chronological sampling of the bodies. Apparently, deaths had decreased, yet the village was nevertheless deteriorating.

It was midmorning when Judy and Mark returned to the village from their early-morning work at the cemetery. And it was then that the trouble began.

As they approached the village, they could see two Vikmoor down at the river relieving two village fishermen of their morning catch. Judy saw no goods being given in trade by the Vikmoor, so she knew this was another example of Vikmoor theft. Two more Vikmoor were standing outside the storage barn, leaning forward on the fence surrounding the adjacent animal pen while they matter-of-factly watched the activity down at the river.

"I don't know how much more of this I can take," Judy said. "Somebody needs to do something to help these people. They need to stand up to these thieves."

"It's none of our business," Mark reminded her.

The path they were on took them quite close to, but past, the wide-open big front door of the barn. As they got closer, they could tell that there were more Vikmoor inside. And they could tell from the tone of the conversation taking place inside that the Vikmoor were making more of their typical demands. Judy decided she wanted to see what was going on, and Mark wanted to learn more about the Vikmoor, so they agreed to cautiously investigate.

Standing just outside the door, they could see that there were three Vikmoor inside arguing with one of the villagers. The Vikmoor were saying that they did not believe that the village was almost out of grain. The villager was saying that that what they saw was all there was, but the Vikmoor kept demanding to know where the rest of the grain was. The villager explained that the season's crop was very poor. It would be barely enough to feed the village. The small crop of grain in the barn was the supply of seed grain, he explained. But the Vikmoor were not satisfied. One of them grabbed the villager by the collar of his tunic and threw him across the room into an empty animal stall.

Judy and Mark were now standing unobtrusively just inside the doorway of the barn. They had not been noticed, and it was a good time to make a quiet retreat, but that's not what happened.

"Hey!" Judy blurted in English. She had had enough. Then in the alien tongue, "He told you that this is all the grain. Can you not see the condition of this place? They will be lucky to make it through winter with what they have."

The villager looked at her with an expression first of surprise, then of confusion.

"That's not our problem, and we know they have more hidden," one of the Vikmoor answered her. "And unless this is your grain, it is not your business."

"We should leave," Mark advised. He turned to go, but Judy held her ground. Mark knew that Judy had not been trained in contact work. Suddenly he became very worried—Judy was still arguing.

"If you take their seed grain, they will have nothing for next year's crop," she continued.

"They have crops in now. They will not starve. They need to work harder. If it does not grow, that is their problem. My people are hungry now."

"Grow your own food."

"Where is your village? Where do you get your food? And what's in your pack? What do you trade?" one of them asked her. She had certainly diverted their attention. But she had done a better job than she bargained for.

One of the aliens suddenly stooped down and started to go through Judy's pack. Mark knew he had to stop them; he could not let them get Judy's gear. He especially did not want to lose the samples and research results.

But before Mark could react, one of the aliens grabbed Judy from behind and put a knife to her throat. Mark made a step forward, but one of the other aliens pushed him back. With his adrenaline pumping, Mark's training began to take over. He exaggerated his backward momentum from the push—buying a second of time—reached into his cloak, and pulled the trigger for his synaptic scrambler at wide field but at two-thirds power; he did not want to get knocked down himself. His back crashed into the wall. The alien stood in front of him and lifted the point of a spear against his throat. Judy still had a knife held to her throat, and she stood frozen, temporarily immobilized by her surprise. The third alien began to go through her pack. A look of excitement came over his face as he ran across Judy's testing equipment. He turned the pack over and dumped the contents onto the ground. But then he stopped and began to look around the room as if he was lost in thought. The room had become still. No one moved. The scrambler was taking over. Just then, the two aliens that had been waiting outside in the bright sun entered into the dark barn. They had heard the activity and wanted to know what was happening. They hesitated as their eyes adjusted to the darkness and they caught a wave of vertigo from the scrambler.

Mark knew that he had to act immediately; with the scrambler set even at two-thirds, it was crossing the spectrum into human. He hoped that the man holding the spear to his throat would by now at least be slowed down by it. Mark swung his left hand up and batted the spear to the side and raised his hood. Simultaneously, he reached into his tunic with his right hand, pulled out his stun gun, and let the two men who had just entered the barn have two quick shots each, and they fell to the ground. The alien holding Judy stood immobilized with his knife still at her throat. She managed to safely sidestep his grasp, and then she fell unconscious to the ground. Mark let her captive have the fifth of his six stun shots.

Mark's mind was groggy from even his limited exposure. He pulled Judy's hood up for her, and despite being nearly incapacitated from the strong feeling of intoxication, he prepared an electrolytic injection for her. Mark pressed the antidote plunger against the meat of her thigh, pushed the plunger home, and knew that the antidote had been safely delivered. By that time, all of the aliens had fallen to the floor and lay in motionless heaps about the room.

Mark knew it was only a matter of time before he and Judy were discovered. He quickly jammed Judy's equipment back into her pack and then gave her some inhalant to help her regain consciousness. Then he went to the door and carefully looked down to the river where the other two aliens were still gathering fish. He heard Judy groaning from the headache caused by the contradictory effects of the scrambler and antidote, and so he knelt down beside her and offered water from his canteen. "Come on, we've got to get out of here." He wiped her face with some of the water. "These guys will be joined by their buddies any minute now."

Judy got up, closed her eyes, shook her head from side to side a couple of times, and then took Mark's canteen and gulped down another mouthful of water. Then she poured some out into her cupped hand and threw the cool water onto her forehead and down across her eyes, face, and neck. "Okay, I'm ready," she said. "Let's go."

"Come on. I'll take your pack." Mark grabbed her pack and led the way out the door. "We'll go up into the hills behind the village. I don't want to chance going anywhere near those other two Vikmoor. We'll walk as fast as we can without making it look like we're running away. I don't want to raise any suspicions."

They walked quickly along the path away from the barn and then turned up the path that headed most directly toward the hills. Mark then looked back and saw that the two Vikmoor that had been at the river were headed up to the barn. Each carried a string of fish and was walking slowly and naturally.

The two astronauts were halfway to the safety of the woods when the two aliens reached the barn. When Mark next looked back, he saw them standing in front of its open door looking around for whomever or whatever it was that had incapacitated their partners. Mark turned to Judy and again told her to walk and act as naturally as possible, but when he again turned and looked over his shoulder, the two aliens were coming at them at a full run, spears in hand. "Come on—run," he yelled in English to the exoarchaeologist, and they both began the run up the base of the hill.

Judy, still under the effects of the scrambler, was having trouble keeping up. Mark paused a second for her to catch up. "You had an awful big dose of that scrambler. Come on, just try to make it to the trees."

She stopped with her hands on her knees, panting. "Sh-t, I screwed up," she said as she tried to catch her breath.

"It's not your fault that you weren't trained for contact."

"Yeah sure, but now what? My head's pounding like my brain's about to explode, and my legs feel like tubes of sand."

"It's the scrambler. Their spectrum is so close to ours that at two-thirds power a lot of it crossed into ours. You're hungover."

The two conscious Vikmoor were racing closer. "Ready? Okay, here's what we'll do. Pull your scrambler trigger at three-quarters long burst mode and drop your cape. At that power, it'll give a good shot but hold it long enough for those guys to catch up to it. We'll keep running and keep it between them and us. If we're lucky, they'll get enough of it to slow them down."

Judy pulled the trigger on her scrambler as the two astronauts again dashed toward the cover of the woods. The two aliens chasing after them were getting so close that it did not take them long to reach the scrambler field. The pursuers kept running. But then one of them slowed down. Feeling that something was wrong, he cocked back his throwing arm to launch his spear. Judy was looking back over her shoulder. "My God," she cried out, stopping and reaching into her cloak, "they're going to throw their spears." She stopped and pulled out her stun gun. "Let's just stop them right here."

"No." Mark turned and tried to stop her but was too late. Judy was already emptying her stun gun at their pursuers. He yelled to her, "They're out of range." The shot did have some effect; it caused a momentary wave of intense nausea that forced both pursuers to stop where they were.

Fighting off the nausea as he best could, one of the men jammed his spear into the ground, unhooked his bow from around his neck, inserted an arrow into the string, pulled it swiftly back, and let loose with an arrow. Almost in unison, the other alien regained enough composure and launched his spear across the sky toward the two astronauts. Time seemed to move in slow motion. Still groggy, Judy stood mesmerized and watched the missiles fly straight toward her.

Mark ran back to her and with his momentum shoved her to one side and kept shoving. He managed to take one step with his right foot, but then the arrow caught him in his upper left leg. "Aaahh," he cried in pain. Judy turned to help him as the spear planted itself into the ground between them. "Go on," he said. "We can't let them get our packs. I don't want to lose our work. Here, take the packs. I'll try to slow them down. I don't think anything's broken." He pulled the barbed arrow all the way through and out the other side. It was a clean wound but bled profusely. "Run! That's an order!" She did. Mark called after her, in English. "I'll meet you at dusk at the cemetery. Call the ship." He pulled up the spear that had missed, cocked back his arm in a throwing position, and pointed the weapon back and forth between the two aliens, who had again started running toward him but now again came to a stop. Mark looked back and saw Judy disappear into the woods. The alien closest to Mark decided to chance an attack and pulled out his long knife and began to charge. Mark pulled out his stun gun and fired his last shot. The alien ran several more paces, and then Mark simply stepped aside and watched him tumble to the ground. Intoxicated by the scrambler and frightened by the weapon, the other alien stayed where he was, slowly loaded another arrow, and fired it straight into Mark's shoulder.

With the second arrow firmly embedded in his shoulder, Mark backed toward the woods as best he could, but he was getting dizzy from the loss of blood, pain, and exhaustion. He stumbled, struggled to catch himself, and fell forward onto the knee of his bad leg. He rolled to his side and then fell back and sat on the ground, the spear slipping from his grasp and falling beside him. He still clutched his stun gun in his left hand, and the remaining attacker, unaware that the gun was empty, kept his distance while loading another arrow, the scrambler now making him move even more slowly, until he collapsed from its effects. For a moment, Mark thought he might escape. But as he looked down the hill, he saw two more Vikmoor running up to join in the attack. It would be impossible to outrun them. So instead of trying to run, he took advantage of the respite, quickly pulled out his knife, cut off a long piece of his cape, and tied a bandage around his leg wound. Then he broke off the arrow in his shoulder as short as he could and packed more bandage around that, but he was still losing blood. As the two reinforcements approached, he picked up the stun gun and pointed it menacingly in their direction, which intimidated and slowed them down. He held his ground as long as he could. He knew if he threw the spear, he could not hope to hit more than one of the attackers, and the other would immediately kill him. He hoped Judy would follow orders and keep running. He felt himself getting weaker. He tried to get up, using the spear as a crutch, but immediately fell forward onto his knees. He steadied himself again one last moment while he looked back to be sure Judy was still in the clear. He collapsed onto his back, looking up at the blue alien sky. He had no strength left to fight. He prayed the end would come quickly.

CHAPTER 14

The Rescue Party

Judy was at home in the forest. When she was a young girl, she and her friends spent much of their summers hiking and exploring the local woods. Then, in undergraduate school, she took a botany class and was forced to spend most of her weekends in the forest collecting specimens. She rediscovered her natural affinity for the forest and felt comfortable there. So it was natural that, like a lot of the astronauts, backpacking became first a hobby and then a passion. So now, instead of thrashing through the forest, she was flying through it. As she ran, she felt and anticipated its obstacles and meanderings as much as a musician might anticipate the next note of even an unfamiliar song. Her body and limbs twisted and curved through, over, around, and underneath the underbrush and trees—twisting away from, over, and through brambles, rocks, logs, and branches without her being consciously aware of them. She ran quickly but quietly without seeming to touch the ground. She blended her natural abilities with the escape and evasion techniques learned in survival school. After sprinting straight into the woods for almost two hundred meters, she cut sharply to her right. Then, coming across a trail that led almost straight away from the village, she raced along it for more than ten minutes before making another right turn and dashing deep into the forest's comforting embrace.

Finally, she felt she could slow down. Now she alternately ran slowly and walked quickly—easing her pace so as to rest while occasionally stopping, only long enough to look and listen for pursuers.

She continued on for almost half an hour, her only rest being the short periods when she slowed to a fast walk. Coming to the edge of a small meadow, she again stopped, looked, and listened, and then hid in a thicket of thorn bushes. She took a small drink from her water ration. Then she removed the heel of her boot, took out her contingency radio, and called the ship.

There was no response to her radio call. The *Cutty*'s orbit put it in position for communication only five minutes out of every ninety. Judy set the all-channel contact signal and switched on the emergency locator beacon.

Eric was the first to respond and learn what had happened.

"It may be awhile before Reggie can get the seclusion he needs to use his radio," Eric surmised. "But the *Cutty* will be overhead soon. I've got the lander about ready to fly. Don't worry; we'll wait and see what the captain says. Try to get some rest."

It was only a matter of minutes before the captain's signal came through.

"Captain, we've got a problem here." Judy quickly described the situation. As they talked, Connors had the starship's resources focus on the new emergency.

"Okay, Judy. We're checking our visual and infrared scanners and don't see anyone near you. One of the Vikmoor is headed away from you and toward the village on the trail you must have been on. I'd say they've given up the search. I'll move the *Cutty* into a synchronous orbit so that we'll be able to keep an eye on things. I'll sign off and get back to you when we've finished the translation. Then we'll find Mark and direct you to a place to camp. Okay?"

"Okay, Captain."

"*Cutty*, out."

"Shore party, out."

Judy again called Eric and had just enough time to update him and eat a nutrient bar when her communicator again signaled an incoming transmission.

"Hello, *Cutty*."

"We found Mark." Connors got immediately to the point. "He's been put in a room at the trading post. We sent him a message through his cranial receiver that we're watching over things, but he hasn't been able to call us back. We'll direct you to a campsite close to the village."

"I'd like to make my way to the top of the hill behind the cemetery. From there I can watch the village, be able to get back into the woods if I have to, and yet be close to where Mark wanted me."

"Okay. Wait ... stand by."

Almost two minutes passed before her captain's signal came back on.

"Judy, I just heard from Eric. The lander's ready. He's going to give it a test hop and then pick up Greene and join you where you are. That meadow's as good a place as any to land. In the meantime, there's a good campsite real close by that I can direct you to. You can rest there. You need it. Does that sound okay? He wanted to convey a sense that the situation was under control, not patronize the science officer. She knew that.

"Yes, Captain."

"Okay, keep your radio on, and we'll direct you to the campsite."

Jake and Eric went through the checklist for liftoff. The first step would be to make a short jump onto the beach. In orbit overhead, Connors and the support crew listened in on the lander's final preparations.

"Okay, Jake, here we go. APU to max. Fan ducts open. Engine switch on. Throttling up. Engage lift fans."

The lander began to rise slowly from the edge of the lake, water pouring from the sides and open wounds of the stricken spacecraft.

"Okay, she's lifting. I'm having some trouble keeping her steady. She's dipping to starboard; I'm correcting to port. No reaction. I'm giving her more to port ... She's rolling halfway over to port, and we're moving laterally along the beach at about forty-five knots. I'm correcting to starboard, no reaction, more to starboard. There she goes halfway to starboard. I'm hitting port, decreasing power to fans. She's sliding along to starboard now, back the way we came but a bit slower. Now she's starting to roll back to port. I'm cutting the fans. Hold on, Jake."

The lander thudded back onto the shore. Despite all of the movement, the flight ended just about where it started.

"Captain, we're okay here, but I really don't know what happened. The auto stabilizers and computers should have evened that ride out, even if I was a little off with the controls. We're down okay, but it was a hard one."

"Is the problem still the computer?"

It was Jake who answered. "I don't think so, Captain. I tested and cannibalized the lifeboat's primary flight computer. Speed and memory all checked out. I know this lifeboat computer can't handle the lander's full-mission autopilot sequencing, but it sure should be able to handle simple stabilization, and that was all it was rigged for. Everything else was switched to manual."

"How about the gyros?"

"All five looked nominal, and so did the computer interface."

"Well, all I can say is we're in a fix. See what you can do. I'm calling Lt. Greene. He'll have to plan on getting to Mark without you."

Greene had known there was an emergency ever since a slightly audible beep came through the nano receiver incorporated into the translator embedded in his skull. He had been in contact with both Judy and the ship and was now just waiting for word of when he would be picked up by Eric. He thought his biggest problem was how to make the rendezvous with the lander without the whole trading party seeing it. He soon heard the beep again and looked for an opportunity to call the ship.

When the trading party stopped for its afternoon water break, Reggie disappeared in the woods as if to relieve himself. He got out his radio and called his captain. Connors told him what happened when Eric had tried to move the lander up onto the beach.

"It sounds like a description of a ham-fisted pilot," was Reggie's response. "But I know that's not true. I'm sure Jake will get to the bottom of it, but for now, Paul and I will make straight for the village. Give me a fix."

Connors gave his lieutenant the current bearing and distance to the village, and then Greene returned to the trading party. He took Paul aside and explained that they would have to head straight and fast to the village. Then he went up to Apsel and told him that he knew the way back to the village from there and that he and Paul would go on by themselves. Partly out of a sense of responsibility for the two Earthmen and partly out of disbelief, Apsel insisted on accompanying them.

They hiked long and hard for the rest of the day, in a straight line through the light underbrush. Apsel said little but looked at his new companions suspiciously as he came to wonder how they navigated without the benefit of compass or marked trails. What he did not know was that Reggie was being directed by the *Cutty*, which zeroed in on his progress with high-resolution scanners and gave him up-to-date course corrections through his implanted receiver. Just as it was getting dark, Reggie was even directed to a perfect campsite. Being able to hike to the edge of nightfall added several hours to their hiking time.

The next morning, Judy sat watching the village. She watched two villagers get conscripted to carry Mark on a stretcher. She saw a woman yanked by force away from the fields and ordered to accompany the Vikmoor party. The force was unnecessary. No resistance was offered as the Vikmoor selfishly appropriated the village's seed grain, poured it into sacks, and put it onto the backs of two more villagers who were drafted as pack bearers. The sun was still low in the morning sky when the Vikmoor troop, complete with its injured captive and slave labor, headed across the river and on toward the Vikmoor village.

Judy was given orders to stay where she was. It was not until late the next day that Reggie and Paul, accompanied by Apsel and the other traders, made it into the village. Judy finally arrived from her hideout and joined the two Earthmen. Reggie introduced her as a fellow traveler from his own village.

They went to the trading post to talk. Reggie saw the man they had seen betrothed sitting at a table close to the bar. He was obviously drunk with ale.

Reggie, Paul, and Judy sat down together around a table farthest from the bar. Apsel joined them. The remainder of their party had gone to the well to get water. Judy updated Reggie with the information that Mark had been carried off as a prisoner.

"We leave immediately," Reggie said. "There are only three of us, but we cannot wait for the others."

"There are four," Apsel added. "I still owe you for the life of Delmar."

"Okay. Four against a troop of Vikmoor—still not good odds," added Paul.

"I know. We could use a few of these villagers. After all, they have been picked on enough; they should be glad to join in," Reggie speculated.

"I doubt we will get any help there," countered Judy. "This is the most passive and apathetic bunch imaginable. No one lifted a hand to stop the abductions of the other villagers, and it has been business as usual ever since."

"I will ask our old buddy over there if anyone can help us," Reggie decided.

Reggie's chair scraped against the wooden floor as he pushed it out from the table and joined their old acquaintance, the young man from the field.

"Remember me?" Reggie asked. "How have you been?"

The alien sat staring at his ale. "How could you ask?" he said. "The Vikmoor have taken my wife. I burn inside with anger. I drink ale to make the anger go away."

"Help us do something about it. One of our friends was taken also. We are going to get him back. We can get your wife, too. You can help."

"We are to turn the other cheek. It is the way. How can you think of violence? We must all set examples to each other."

"We believe a similar way, but we do not turn from helping others. We will help your wife and the other prisoners. They do not want to be kept by the Vikmoor, do they?"

"No. My wife, Mahria, she will kill herself; she has said so before. But she will not lose herself to violence."

"Then help us help her. Maybe it is not too late. Help us gather the rest of the villagers to chase down the Vikmoor and get all of our friends back."

"No. Violence is not to be met with violence. Anger and hatred solve nothing. Self-sacrifice shows the strength and proof of our beliefs."

"It is not self-sacrifice to let others get hurt. The sacrifice is to help them. Is peace your only goal? Do you sacrifice all to prove that peace is to be had at all costs? Your peace is routinely broken by these Vikmoor raids. There is no sign it will ever end. Is that really peace? We see a difference between good and evil and believe that evil must be corrected. To preserve peace without giving into evil, action must sometimes be taken."

At that point, Judy joined them. "Come on, Reggie, this is no use. We have to do it on our own."

Reggie went back to their table. The villager went to the bar to get more ale to dull his mind and returned to his own table.

"I cannot ask my men to come," Apsel continued. "War is a terrible thing, and they could get the sickness. But I will join you."

"Okay," said Reggie. "We will leave just before dawn. I want to get on the move. I wonder why they took him anyway."

"Maybe just to punish him for fighting," Apsel said. "Or maybe for profit—to sell him back to you."

The sharp splintering sound of a breaking ale glass suddenly shattered the quiet. Reggie turned to see his seemingly apathetic acquaintance sitting with the crushed remains of an ale mug in his now bleeding hands. The villager sat glassy eyed, staring at his hands and broken mug.

"Do not tell me he is not angry," said Reggie.

"I hope not," answered Apsel, "or he will surely die. The gods will punish him. But I have already done so many bad things in my life; I am sure the gods already plan on punishing me. I will help you get your friend."

Well, okay, Apsel, I thank you. Your help I value greatly. I am sure it will make a difference. Come. Let us see if there is anything here we can use."

Apsel followed Reggie to the trading portion of the inn. The storekeeper had been listening and was immediately attentive. "We could use those gas bombs," said Reggie.

"It's okay," Apsel told the storekeeper. "I will tell my people that I took them." The storekeeper recognized Apsel as one of the Hill People and so turned over the requested gas bombs.

"What is in those canisters?" Reggie asked, pointing to four one-liter ceramic jars.

"Oil for lanterns. I will let you have them at a good price."

"Okay, I will trade you this cooking equipment for one of them." Reggie placed the mess kit from Mark's backpack on the counter.

"I don't think so. What else can you give me?"

Reggie sweetened the deal with some fishing line, buttons, and the compass that he had traded for. The shopkeeper still hesitated. Reggie preferred not to steal items he could trade for, so he continued to bargain. He knew from survival school that nothing should be discarded—a use for it would certainly arise—so he hated to trade anything away, but he felt that the oil was something he should not pass up.

"Here, I will throw in these fish hooks and this hunting knife if you throw in a few bottles of whiskey." Reggie put the offered items up on the counter and pointed to a row of whiskey bottles. The shopkeeper agreed, put out two bottles of whiskey and a liter of lantern fuel, and they closed the trade. Reggie put the goods in his pack.

Thinking that the shopkeeper would have some influence over the villagers, Reggie asked him to help recruit for the rescue party but was refused. "Violence is not the way of peace," was the unsurprising response.

"Okay, just rent us a room."

The astronauts went upstairs while Apsel told his men to complete the trading mission without him. Then he joined the astronauts in the single room they would share for the few hours of sleep Reggie had allotted them.

It was five in the morning when Reggie awakened them. They dressed, repacked their gear, and went down to the inn for breakfast. There they were met by Apsel's three trading partners, who announced that they would not let Apsel go without them. They had decided to go along. They all sat down to breakfast together. Reggie now trusted the food from experience as well as from the lab tests. Nothing harmful had been found, and supplies were running low, so the astronauts ate the same as the others. But due to the Vikmoor pillaging, the innkeeper had little food to offer. Some moldy cheese, stale dark bread, and thick dark coffee served as breakfast.

The young man whose wife had been stolen was still sitting at his table with a drink in his hand. He sat staring into the now cold hearth of the fireplace, his back to the bar. Reggie decided to try once more to recruit his help. Surely, Reggie thought, this man should want to join an endeavor that could rescue his young wife, and he must have friends and family who would want to join in. Reggie walked up to him and tried to get his attention, but the alien's blank stare could not be broken. Apsel joined them.

"It is the sleeping sickness," Apsel explained. "Soon he will pass out. An evil heart is the heart of death. His anger still burns in him. Next, the sores will come. I have seen it before. In a week, he will be dead. Come, let us get going."

They returned to their table, finished eating, and then the party of seven set off toward the Vikmoor village. The sun was just beginning to shine through the trees at the top of the hill across the river. A thin mist of fog that still blanketed the water muffled the sounds of the oars banging against the wooden sides of the boats as the rescuers rowed their way to the landing on the river's far bank. There they began their journey up the trail that followed the course of the river toward the Vikmoor village.

They soon reached the spot where Reggie and Mark had incapacitated the first two test subjects. Reggie told the others to go ahead, and he made a detour to the old observation camp. He had decided to stop at the camp to get extra power packs for the stun guns and food rations from the cache of supplies they had left hidden there. He also wanted some privacy from Apsel for contacting the ship. He knew it was time to talk to his captain to discuss rescue plans. He was glad he did.

"We're pretty sure we have the Vikmoor village spotted, Reggie. You're not going to be able to catch up to Mark before they get there, and extracting him from that village is going to be a real challenge. It's well defended, with guard towers and barbed wire around the entire perimeter. It has about two hundred residents, not counting any that may be on their way in from patrols. It looks like you could use some help, but it would take another week for Eric and Jake to hike there, and I don't want to send down another lifeboat."

"I agree, Captain. If the Poplarville beam system tries to switch on to take shots at something, my sabotage job may be discovered. I'd rather not give their technicians a chance to fix it before we try to leave. With the condition our lander will be in, I don't want to have to try to dodge that beam when we try to make orbit. Besides, we may still need Poplarville's cooperation, and that would be harder to get if they guessed that I sabotaged their equipment.

"We'll have to come up with something on our own. I've been through Mark's exoanthropology kit. Fortunately Judy was able to salvage it with the rest of Mark's pack, and it has some pretty good stuff—two smoke grenades, the synaptic scrambler, a small bottle of super caustic, and two small explosive grenades."

"It's part of his infiltration gear."

"Well, I'm glad to have it. Plus we each have our own gear. And I've got a handful of those mustard gas bombs. I guess they'll get a taste of their own medicine. I think we're in pretty good shape."

"Good. By the time you get there, we should have more intelligence on the layout of the village for you. If I absolutely have to, I'll send down a whole lifeboat full of all the weapons you can carry. I haven't lost a landing party yet, and I don't intend to start now. It would look bad on my efficiency report."

They terminated the communication, and Reggie hurried to catch up with Apsel and the rest of the rescue party.

When Reggie caught up to them, he realized they had stopped to rest and give him a chance to catch up. He decided he needed to take the opportunity to have an important talk with Apsel.

"Apsel, I've been thinking about this. The sleeping sickness does not sound like it's a complete myth. Your cousin has definitely found evidence that there is something real to it. I may not understand it, but I have to acknowledge it. Maybe you should not come with us."

"I know, friend, but like I said before, the gods already have ample reason to take me. They may as well do it now. You saved the life of one of my people. You helped us return with the food from my trading mission, so you could say you helped feed my village. I have learned something from you. I have learned that sacrifice sometimes means more than surrendering. And it means something different than simply not fighting others. Now one of your people is in danger. I must help you."

"Well, thank you, Apsel, but maybe you better release your men."

"I tried, but they have all been on many profitable trading missions with me, and they suspect that this may yet prove to be a profitable trip. Their motives are purely personal. I think perhaps they do not truly understand the danger."

Reggie had to respect Apsel's loyalty. Apsel knew the risks of the disease and had to have some fear that combat would kill him. But he seemed as cold and professional as the Earthmen. There was no talk of revenge. There was little talk of death. Just talk of helping others as Apsel had been helped by the Earthmen.

The Vikmoor were slowed down by Mark's stretcher, and Reggie was able to travel by night as well as by day. He was less than one day behind when the Vikmoor reached their village.

Reggie pushed the team hard that last day. They hiked well into the night and then slept until just before dawn. Then, after just a two-hour march, Reggie led them off the trail and through some light underbrush, over a low hill and down into a long, grassy meadow. He had been guided by the *Cutty*. From its synchronous orbit, the hostages were constantly monitored and the rescuers' progress directed. Directions and informational updates were continuously fed to Reggie through the receiver in his implanted translator/ receiver. So far, he had managed to maintain the subterfuge that he was from a village little different than Poplarville. Reggie knew, however, that Apsel would think differently after the equipment was deployed.

"Prepare your men, then sleep. The Vikmoor are just a three-hour hike away. Today we will rest. Tonight we will study them. Tomorrow night, we attack."

As Apsel left to prepare his men, he admitted to himself that the word "attack" had frightened him. It really drove home what they were about to do—fight! Hurting other people. But what had to be done had to be done. It was no different from building the gas bombs. Sometimes there were accidents, and workers were killed, but it was work that had to be done. He gave his men one last chance to leave, but none took it.

Apsel went back to where Reggie was sitting and was stunned to find him speaking with someone through a wireless telephone.

His mind occupied by the rescue, Reggie had made a careless mistake in getting caught using the radio. But just as Reggie began to condemn himself, he realized that secrecy no longer mattered. Apsel would learn the truth about Reggie's people soon enough. Care in planning and executing the mission must now take priority. Reggie barely looked up from the communicator as he continued his conversation with his captain. Reggie was receiving a complete description of the camp and was planning a reconnaissance mission.

Although Reggie knew that the description he was being given would be invaluable, he also knew it would not be enough to conduct the rescue operation. For that, he knew that a firsthand reconnaissance of the village was necessary. And such a reconnaissance would be the closest thing they could have to a training mission. One thing astronauts had in common with commandos was a penchant for rehearsing every step and contingency of every task and mission. And this would be very much a commando mission.

Apsel tried to act nonchalant about the wireless telephone. He told Reggie his men were ready, and Reggie shared his plans for the reconnaissance. Then they all took turns sleeping or staying awake at watch. Reggie wanted everyone to rest that day and begin the reconnaissance shortly after nightfall. It was not to be.

CHAPTER 15

The Vikmoor Village

Mark rested quietly on a cot in the small room provided by his captors. His cape and personal gear had been taken. The door and windows were blocked with metal bars. He was alone.

He had been carried on a stretcher by the other prisoners all the way to the Vikmoor village. The march had been pressed but not hurried. His Vikmoor guards hiked purposely but did not fear pursuit and frequently rested. Cook fires were built at night, but the few portions of food Mark was given were apparently an afterthought. He was not mistreated but simply treated as cargo. Surprisingly to him, so was the woman prisoner. Apparently she was brought to help with personal chores rather than favors. Later he would learn that they both had been taken for barter and that they were to be, for the time being, undamaged. Mark tried to keep track of her. He was confident that his crewmates would pull him out, and he was not going to leave her or any of the other Anacondans behind.

Mark had received several messages over the ship to the shore receiver built into the translator/receiver embedded in his skull. He wished it included a transmitter and hoped that he would be given a chance to get out his contingency radio, but at least he knew that Reggie and the others were just half a day behind.

He got up and struggled to make it to the widow, dragging his injured leg across the concrete floor. He was standing there testing the bars when he heard a door open and clang shut at the end of the hallway. That was followed by the echoing steps and muffled conversation of several of his captors coming toward his cell. He could not hear them clearly enough to understand what they were saying, but he could tell that they stopped at the woman's cell, exchanged words, and began laughing before continuing toward his cell. He limped back to his cot and was lying on his back with his hands behind his head staring at the ceiling when one of the Vikmoor guards appeared at his cell door window.

He heard the metallic click of the lock, and the door swung open. Wordlessly, two Vikmoor grabbed him under the arms and pulled him up against the wall, while a third stood in front of him watching.

"You have had enough time to think," the third man began. "Tell us where your village is."

"I am a trader from beyond the long lake—" Mark began, but before he could finish his interrogator reached down and dug a finger through the bandage and into the hole in his injured leg, down to the bone. The pain was sharp and deep. The air in his lungs involuntarily burst out of him in a cry of surprise and pain.

"You are lying," said the man.

Mark was trying to get his breath. He tried to talk but could not force enough air from his lungs to form words. The alien removed his finger from the wounded leg. Mark stood pinned against the wall and tried to fill his lungs with huge gulps of air.

"Speak the truth," the third man continued. "We know you are from the Hill People."

"No, I swear," Mark answered. Again the finger was dug deep into his leg wound. Then, again he was given time to breathe and reconsider his answer.

"Tell us the way to your village."

"I speak the truth. We came here to trade." Mark then saw a fourth man enter the room.

"He may be speaking the truth. Why did you not ask him these questions before you brought him here?" the newcomer asked.

"We wanted to get away from the village before his people came. Now, even if he will not answer us, we are safe and can trade him back to the Hill People, or maybe follow them back to their village after they come for him. Then we can take what we need."

"What if he is telling the truth?"

"We have nothing to lose by trying. This man fought us. His partner escaped. They shot us with some kind of new weapon and used something to put us to sleep. If he is not Hill People, we need to learn more about his real village. Either way, we may be able to trade him for goods. We can question him more later." He turned back to his two strongmen. "Release him." Mark slid to the floor.

With a jerk of his head, the interrogator led his two partners from the room. The newcomer remained. He stood there for a moment looking at Mark as the astronaut stared blankly forward.

"Oleif will be back," he said to Mark, which caused Mark to look up at him.

"My name is Hugin. I am one of the trustees here, but so is Oleif. He will not leave you alone for long. He knows we need the food. For that, we need information about your village. We will ask your people for a fair trade—nothing more. Tell me, and I will save you from this. But I cannot help you if you do not tell me the truth about where you are from."

"I have told the truth."

"I do not believe you, and I can help you only if you help me. Now, what is the way to your village?"

"I told you, we are from beyond the long lake."

Hugin walked over and stood looking through the window toward the early morning sun. "You do not understand. I do not believe you, and I really have little sympathy for you. You should have minded your own business in the village. We need food. That is all Oleif's men wanted. Why you interfered, I do not understand. Your people have plenty. You have always had plenty. When the time of chaos came, you had your machines and your knowledge. Others had land—or at least were welcomed by those who did—and they began to grow food. My people were trapped here. When we tried to go out to join farms, we were chased away. We were all just a bunch of criminals not to be trusted and not to be worried about, they said. We went back in larger numbers and ready for trouble. 'Okay then, give us food,' we demanded and took what we needed. We were used to taking what we wanted anyway. After all, that is how most of our people had gotten here. You forced us into this by trapping us here and giving us nothing. That was a long, long time ago, the time of my great-grandfather. But it was that way then, and it is that way now."

"You have plenty of land here. Grow your own food. My people will show you how. There is no need to steal."

"You may call it stealing. To us, it is surviving. We had been locked up here with nothing. Grow our own food? Look out at the trees. None are older than I. The land was poisoned so that nothing would grow around us so there would be nothing to hide an escape. Then the war came, and we were left with no food and the land poisoned. We were stuck here in this land of death. No way to grow our own food, and the other villages would not accept us."

"There is plenty of unclaimed land beyond this camp."

"Oh, we have tried to grow crops on ground not poisoned, but the animals get them, or we plant at the wrong time, or they get not enough water or too much water. None of us are farmers. So we take what we need.

"Now, where is your village? Maybe we can trade *you* for the things we need."

"I told you, but also I will warn you. If you do not release me, my people will come for me."

"We are ready for that."

"But we can help you. Fight us, and you will get hurt."

"Help us like so many have helped us in the past?"

"It can be different this time."

"I have no reason to trust you, or to want to trust you, and we do not want your charity. No. We will take what we need.

"I did not come here to argue with you. There is nothing to argue about. If you do not tell me where your village is, and if your people do not trade for you, there will be nothing I can do for you. Then Oleif can have you. Today you will be left alone. Tomorrow, Oleif will start his interrogation. I will come back tomorrow morning to see if you have changed your mind. Then I will leave you with Oleif. Do you understand?"

"Yes."

Hugin turned and left the room, locking the barred door behind him. Mark slowly got up and limped to his bunk. He could hear the girl softly sobbing somewhere down the hall.

He waited until the door slammed closed at the end of the hall, signaling the departure of the interrogator. Then he continued his fruitless inspection of the cell. He had wanted to wait until dark before removing the contingency radio hidden in his boot heel. But it would be unwise to wait. Oleif's interrogation would not be a picnic. Mark decided to call the *Cutty* to see if he could speed up the timing of his rescue.

CHAPTER 16

Attempted Rescue

The nine-acre Vikmoor village was surrounded by a rusting barbed-wire-topped chain-link fence. At each corner of the village's square perimeter stood a concrete, three-story-tall guard tower. Three of the village's sides had an additional tower at the midpoint between corners. On the fourth side, the west side, two such towers flanked a central gate. The village itself consisted of a number of long two-story, redbrick, flat-roofed buildings. A separate building stood just inside the front gate but was fenced off from the rest of the village by a second fence and central gate. A number of Vikmoor could be seen moving about the village.

Reggie and his accomplices were on the crest of the southern of the three hills that surrounded the forested floor of the isolated box canyon, in the center of which stood the Vikmoor village. They lay on their stomachs, passing a powerful visi-scope back and forth between them, peering through the trees at their target. To their left, the valley opened up into a narrow floodplain, beyond which was the river that flowed down to Anaconda. An ancient roadway, now no more than a footpath, led from the direction of the river and up to the gates at the village's western perimeter. The sun had nearly reached its zenith, and the village looked stark and hot in its short-shadowed midday glare.

An early-morning communication from the *Cutty Sark* had altered the rescuers' plans. Having been contacted and advised of the situation by Mark, Connors had become alarmed by the foreboding promise of Mark's next interrogation. Connors therefore requested an immediate assault. Reggie did not like it; he regretted the inability to carefully plan and rehearse the mission, but he agreed with his captain that there was no choice.

Reggie was the first with the visi-scope. "It looks to me like there must be at least two hundred people living there." He passed the instrument to Apsel.

"No crop lands," Apsel noted. "And I know of nothing they trade. Just as I heard, they take all their food from others." Apsel passed the scope back to Reggie.

"And no parade grounds. No sign of an armory or defensive bulwarks—just that barbed-wire-topped chain-link fence." Reggie passed the visi-scope to Paul.

"The facilities all look original, a lot like the ones at Apsel's village," Paul noted.

"It probably hasn't changed much since before the war," Reggie agreed. "But why did they go to all the trouble of building those guard towers and then just build chain-link fences?"

"Our secure areas are much the same way, Reggie. We don't build forts anymore," Paul reminded him and passed the instrument to Judy.

She lay there for a few moments contemplating what she saw. Then ... "Look, the barbed-wire sections at the top of the fence were made to angle in, not out. That angle is designed to keep something in, not keep something out. And all of the buildings except that one in front that's fenced off from the others have bars on all the windows, and even that one has them on one end of the first floor. It was probably the administration building. I think this was a prison." She passed the visi-scope back to Paul, who took a quick look and passed it on to Reggie.

"You may be right," Reggie said. "You know, I think I may be starting to understand this planet," he slipped. Apsel gave him a quick glance. "All the more reason to get my exoanthropologist out of there," Reggie continued. "Here is what we will do ..."

Reggie had briefly toyed with the idea of trying to trade for Mark. There was a risk that some of the Vikmoor would get killed in the attack, and the Service tried to avoid that sort of thing. But he feared he did not have enough to trade. And besides, he could not be sure that the Vikmoor could be trusted. A surgical strike was the only answer, and the element of surprise was important to the mission's success. Although the Service preferred to preserve alien cultures so that they could develop and be studied unaltered, this was different. The whole planet had suffered a major catastrophe and needed to be helped, not abandoned to its own fate. He decided he would risk the dangers of a rescue by force.

Reggie laid out his plan.

They worked quickly. Reggie was determined to have everything ready and a new base camp established well before dark so that they could rest before the attack. They were slowed down, however, by the challenge of remaining undiscovered.

First, they dug a deep but short slit trench for Paul at the crest of the hill at the top southern side of the U that formed the valley's open mouth. That end of the valley was well forested with old growth forest. From that vantage point, the opening to the valley could be easily observed and defended. Sitting there, Paul could see the junction of the trail from the Vikmoor village and the main trail that followed the river and in one direction led to Anaconda. To his left, the floodplain was so narrow that the river was barely beyond a hundred meters away. The trail that followed the river was about a third of that distance. But Paul's position was well concealed and would be impossible to see in the dark. While the hole was being dug, Judy scouted and partially cleared an escape path. The rescuers were concealed in their work by the thick growth of the forest and with the aid of the ever-watching eye of the unseen *Cutty Sark*, which was parked overhead in its synchronous orbit. With the *Cutty* watching over them, they were given ample warning before anyone traveled near them on the nearby trail. And because the starship's scanners had no trouble painting a complete picture of the interior of every building in the compound, the rescue party was provided with exact intelligence regarding Mark's prison—a holding cell in the administration building.

Finally, Reggie circled back up to the west side of the camp, crept through the new growth trees as close as he could, crawled until he was just sixty meters from the main gate and its dual towers, and set up the synaptic scrambler. He would have liked to position it closer, but with the two extra towers on that side, he was afraid the odds were just too high that he would be spotted there. He switched the scrambler on, tuned it, pocketed the remote, and slowly backed away. It was too far away to put anyone to sleep, so instead he had tuned it so that it would disrupt the brain functions with something similar to a feedback loop. Although the village was outside the field unit's optimum range, having it on all day would have a cumulative unsteadying effect. He hoped that it would at least cause nausea to the point of keeping the guards distracted from their posts. Reggie was not as well trained with the equipment as Mark was, but with the aid of instructions radioed down from the *Cutty Sark*, he thought he could get the job done. Mark would not be affected at the selected setting, and being directed toward the camp, the exposure of Apsel and his men would be limited.

After positioning the scrambler and scouting escape routes, Reggie led his team back to their temporary camp. There, Reggie made their final preparations. One of Apsel's men was a bowman, and Reggie wrapped some of his arrows with cloth stripped from extra clothing and instructed him to douse them with lamp oil just before attacking. Next, Reggie emptied the two liquor bottles, filled them with lamp oil, and loosely stuffed in a wick made of more cloth. Then they all ate and bedded down for several hours of sleep.

At 0400 local time, a time of night when the guards could be expected to be the most unaware, the attack began. Reggie carried the mustard gas bomb he had stolen from Poplarville, a better than 75 percent charge on his personal scrambler, his stun gun, a vial of super caustic, two smoke bombs, two explosive grenades, and Paul's core drill. Paul was in his position above the trail junction with two of the mustard gas bombs purchased at Anaconda and his stun gun. Judy carried her own stun gun and wore Paul's cape with its scrambler. One of Apsel's men carried a bow and the flammable arrows; the other two each carried a mustard gas bomb. Apsel carried one of the gas bombs, and like his men, he also had his long knife. In addition to their other weapons, Judy and Apsel each carried one of the liquor bottle firebombs. Reggie and Judy led them through the woods and then through the new growth forest that surrounded the village.

Reggie was counting on two things to distract the Vikmoor defense. First was the timing of the attack. Reggie felt fairly confident that the Vikmoor would not anticipate how prompt the response to the kidnapping would be. Another element of the timing was the early-morning hour of the attack, which Reggie hoped would help catch the defenders off balance. Second, Reggie hoped that the scrambler would debilitate many of the Vikmoor. The field unit was not powerful enough to affect the whole village, so he had set it up so that it was concentrated on the defenses at the main gate. There was a chance that it would even affect the guards in the administration building, although to a lesser extent. The symptoms would change only as to degree. As set, the scrambler would have a cumulative effect, creating a general nausea very similar to motion sickness. Those most strongly affected would be practically bedridden. Even its less powerful effects could create a debilitating nausea such that the victim would be reluctant to sit or stand, much less undertake strenuous activity. It could take a great deal of initiative for one of its victims to move about. Furthermore, the waves of nausea could in the very least be so overpowering that they would preoccupy and divert the victim's normal thinking.

Still unseen, Judy, Apsel, and Reggie burst out of the woods at the southwest corner of the compound and silently ran straight for the main gate. Reggie dissolved its lock with super caustic, swung it open, and ran past the outer building in the administration area and up to the inner gate. The squeaking of the first gate swinging open roused the gate tower guards, but they were all impaired by the synaptic scrambler. One sat on the floor with his head in his hands. Others were curled on the floor. Only one got up, but as he reached for his bow, he tripped over a bucket of vomit. Reggie pushed the inner gate closed as tightly as he could and positioned the core sampler hard against it. Then he firmly and quickly drove the core sampler deep into the ground by firing the explosive charge used to drive the sampler into bedrock. That would effectively block the gate shut, isolating the administration building from the rest of the village. There was still no response from the inner village as Reggie pulled the pin on his mustard gas bomb and lobbed it over the top of the inner gate—thereby helping ensure the isolation of the administration area from the main compound. He turned and ran halfway to the administration building in the five seconds it took the bomb to explode. In those five seconds, Apsel and Judy had lit their firebombs and hurled them into the base of the gate towers just as the guards forced themselves up and began ringing the alarm bells. At the same time, Apsel's archer began shooting fire arrows into the south-central and southwest guard towers to add to the general confusion.

Reggie was almost to a side window of the administration building when Vikmoor guards began streaming out of its front door. Apsel headed straight for them, counting ten of them before he threw his mustard gas bomb at them. He used the shortest time delay that he dared. He was turning back when a determined gate tower guard let loose with a badly aimed arrow that easily missed. By this time, all of Apsel's men were in the compound, and the bowman pinned down the single threatening tower guard with three quick shots of his own. This gave Apsel the time he needed to get away, and as he reached Judy, she fired off five shots with her stun gun, dropping five of the guards who were regrouping and circling around the fog of Apsel's mustard gas. Apsel's bowman, the bloodlust of battle driving him on, finally got off a clean shot that killed the tower guard that he had just missed, then spun around and put fatal shots into three of the defenders trying to make an end run around the mustard gas.

Flames in the gate towers had reached the upper decks, and guards were jumping to the ground in desperation and panic. With more guards now cutting Apsel and the others off from where Reggie was at the administration building, Apsel signaled to retreat toward the river. The Vikmoor took off after them.

Unnoticed yet separated from the others by the stiffening Vikmoor defense, Reggie leaped through the administration building's side window and landed in a bunkroom emptied by the commotion. He watched his people race down the trail away from the compound with a swarm of Vikmoor guards in hard pursuit.

Opening the door into the hallway was easy. The building had been emptied of its guards. Apparently they had left to chase off the attackers—just as Reggie had hoped and planned. Reggie knew the exact layout of the building from the reconnaissance provided by the *Cutty Sark* and went straight to Mark's room. Alerted via his cranial receiver that the rescue was coming, Mark was not surprised when he saw Reggie standing in the open doorway—the super caustic again having speedily done its job. Mark was in excruciating pain from his injury and interrogation, but he was able to walk. They made their way down the hall and stopped and got the girl. She was so startled by all of the commotion that it took some persuading to get her to go with them. And with her helping to support Mark, they hobbled out the front door, rescuing the other two captives on the way.

The gate tower guards were no longer a threat. Those who could chased Apsel's group; the others were too incapacitated by their injuries. However, the mustard gas clouds at the inner gate were dissipating, and the Vikmoor inside were pushing and bending the gate open far enough to slip through one at a time. Three who had squeezed through had been running toward the main gate and had just reached the administration building when they saw Reggie and headed straight for him. Stopping for a moment, Reggie lobbed one of his explosive grenades. That terminated that threat. Now they raced on for the main gate with Mark practically suspended between Reggie and the girl. Now three more guards who had slipped through from the inner compound came running at them. One of those guards stopped and raised a bow to let loose an arrow. Reggie, despite one of Mark's arms being draped around his neck, twisted around, took quick aim while continuing to run, and let loose with two shots from his stun gun. Neither was a clean hit, but one grazed and stunned the bowman enough that his arrow flew clear. The other two guards— not having stopped to fire—were now right up on them. Passing Mark to one of the men he'd just rescued, Reggie let loose with two more shots, and those two guards fell to the ground. The third guard was coming on fast as Reggie led the escapees out through the main gate. As more pursuers came up from behind, Reggie punched the synaptic scrambler's remote to maximum output while turning and throwing a smoke grenade. The scrambler used the last of its remaining power in one final sustained burst that dropped their pursuers to their knees in uncontrollable waves of vertigo. They would be down for mere seconds, but it would be time enough. Now, hidden by the smoke but with the aid of his goggles set for night vision, Reggie led the escapees into the woods, following a route he had scouted when placing the scrambler. They were pulling Mark along at a full run and were soon notified by the *Cutty* that no one was following them. The guards who were managing to get their wits about them were leaderless and taking no chances; they were simply falling into defensive positions at the gate.

Farther down the main trail, Judy let Apsel and the others run ahead while she engaged her scrambler and dropped her cape. The scrambler field trimmed the mob of pursuers down to ten before its power was drained and stragglers trampled past it.

Paul could tell from the orange glow of the flames coming from the direction of the village that the attack had begun. So he was sitting and watching carefully with his night-vision goggles as Apsel, his three men, and Judy came running down the trail and sped off to the left toward Anaconda. The Vikmoor guards had not managed to catch up with them. Judy's scrambler had slowed down the guards that it had not put down.

Apsel, his men, and Judy did not pause to look up to Paul as they turned out of the valley and headed down the trail toward Anaconda, dispersing the last of their mustard gas as they ran. Soon, their Vikmoor pursuers rounded the same corner but at a somewhat slower pace as they approached the gas field and from the lingering effects of the scrambler. Led now by Judy in her night-vision goggles, her team had no trouble keeping up a fast pace as they raced down the trail.

Paul watched the Vikmoor disappear down the trail. On that narrow floodplain, the two bombs he had would be sufficient to totally seal off the trail, but he could see that they were unnecessary—there was no sign of additional

Vikmoor guards. The *Cutty* was watching from orbit and soon confirmed that the guards were not trying to catch Judy and Apsel's team. The pursuers had been blocked by the final disbursement of mustard gas. Dispirited, the Vikmoor were now slowly headed slowly back toward their village and were no longer a threat to anyone. It was also confirmed that no one else from the village was pursuing Reggie. Paul would not have to team up with him, and Judy and Apsel would not have to double back in support.

Besides the element of surprise, the rescuers had been aided by the fact that most of the villagers were incapacitated by the scrambler or were fast asleep. The guards who were posted were there more out of tradition than real expectation of attack. The villagers lacked military training and advanced planning. So it was more of a mob than a concerted defense that had opposed the rescue party.

The diversion and rescue had been a success. Reggie had planned it as a variation of an ancient strategy. Judy and Apsel had feigned a retreat, pulling their foe with them, and had fallen back to below Paul's prepared position. From there they could have met and defeated their pursuers. Then they would have raced up the hill and doubled back to meet Reggie while he raced through the woods toward them. Now, having learned from the *Cutty* that that all was well, Reggie flashed up an infrared beacon as a final signal to make for the primary rendezvous.

Mark was safe.

CHAPTER 17

The Plague

Paul withdrew from his position as soon as he saw the beacon. He flashed up an answering beacon and retreated along the path that had been cleared by Judy and was soon met by Reggie on the same path. The two beacons were plainly visible in Judy's night-vision goggles, and she sent up her own answering beacon. The beacons painted a good picture to everyone of all of their positions and communicated more immediately than radio contact would have.

Reggie's group was the first to get to the rendezvous. Reconnaissance provided by the orbiting starship confirmed to the lieutenant that the rescue teams were not being followed.

A tint of blue sky had already stretched across the eastern horizon before Judy led the rest of the rescue party back into camp. Reggie had coffee and a breakfast of chemically heated survival rations waiting for them when they arrived. They would rest while they ate and then get moving. He expected the Vikmoor to chase them in force. There was no time for celebrating, only for a round of hugs and handshakes among the reunited astronauts, in which Apsel and his men joined. Then they all huddled together in a circle to eat, despite being so emotionally and physically drained from the battle and its preparations that no one was hungry. The survival rations were tasteless enough that the aliens noticed nothing unusual. After eating, Reggie told them they had twenty minutes to get organized and rest before heading back to Anaconda.

Reggie knew that the Vikmoor had enough people to cover every trail leading from their village. But with the *Cutty Sark* keeping track of Vikmoor activity, he knew he could keep clear of them. So he kept to the main trail. They made very good time.

It was still early morning, and fires still burned, and wounded still lay where they had fallen when the Vikmoor made their first move. Reggie received word of it from space.

"Reggie, this is *Cutty Sark*." It was the starship's captain. "It looks like the Vikmoor are up to something. A mob of about fifty armed men is on the march along the main trail to Anaconda. They're not really searching the woods or trying to find your trail."

"Roger, Captain. Stand by." Reggie turned to Apsel, and they hurriedly discussed the Vikmoor movements. Then Reggie called back up to the ship.

"Captain, we're afraid the Vikmoor plan on taking out their revenge on Anaconda. Or maybe they just want to start from there to search for Poplarville. Either way, Anaconda is the place to stop them. We're going to have to defend that village. We need to beat them there. How does our trail look?"

"There's a group of about five Vikmoor headed your way from Anaconda. And the group that just left their village is about two hours behind you."

"Okay. The guys coming from Anaconda can't know what just happened, but I don't want to take any chances.

Those guys are too likely to harass us just to steal our supplies."

"You've got a good head start on the group behind you. We'll give you time to duck and cover from anything else."

"True, but we'll need time to prepare some defenses once we get there, and we could use some help. The lander's less than a two-day march from there. I'm going to have Eric meet us there. I delayed calling him in because I want that lander fixed, but it looks like I'm going to need him. I'll get back to you, Captain."

Reggie radioed his second in command. "Eric, there's a mob of fifty armed men marching on Anaconda. We're going to have to defend the village. I want Jake to keep working on the lander and Elizabeth to keep working on her research, but I want you to join us there."

Eric hesitated. He knew it was a break in protocol to travel alone.

"Don't worry, Eric," Reggie continued. "The *Cutty* can keep an eye on you from orbit. And you'll be wearing the next best thing to combat armor. I want you to wear one of the survival suits. Those things can stand up to a lot of punishment, so you should be pretty safe. It can at least stand up to anything the Vikmoor can throw at you. I also want you to bring all the stun grenades you can carry. And bring the rocket gun and a mortar. Also, plenty of extra power packs for the stun guns. And you'd better bring a laser rifle. The suit's servo assists should make it easy to carry the load."

Reggie kept up a fast march all that day and through early evening. He was able to travel almost a half day's march farther than the Vikmoor, who lacked the advantages of night-vision goggles and satellite reconnaissance. Apsel's bowman wanted to turn and fight, but they pressed on.

It was only after a full two days of this forced march that Reggie felt they were far enough ahead of the Vikmoor attack party that they could stop to camp for more than a shortened sleep break. Now that they were getting close, he wanted everyone to have some time to eat a hot meal, mend their gear, rest, and sleep. He wanted them to be in good shape when they reached Anaconda. It was then that he noticed that one of Apsel's men, the bowman, was getting sores like the ones Apsel had attributed to the sleeping sickness.

Apsel confirmed the diagnosis, and Reggie called Elizabeth by radio. He explained to her that he believed there was a connection between violent behavior and the disease. He asked her to investigate.

"See what it is. Send the UAS, and we'll send you samples for analysis. We should be in range now. Call in the *Cutty* for analysis help."

The small robot plane arrived just after dawn. The thick forest canopy prevented landing. Instead, the robot made a low pass and dropped a pickup kit. Then it circled the camp until a bright red balloon with the sample canister suspended beneath it lifted slowly into the morning sky. The robot then turned and flew straight into the suspension line. The capture gear latched onto it, cut the balloon loose, and pulled the canister up into the robot for transport to the lander. Again, Apsel saw that these new friends were very different.

Shortly thereafter, Elizabeth was able to start an analysis of the sample. Data links to the *Cutty Sark* facilitated the data processing and analysis. Elizabeth was confident that she now had enough information to isolate the disease—if it was real. She had a sample from a sick subject, healthy subjects, and biopsies obtained at the cemetery from subjects who had evidently died earlier of unrelated causes; one had a broken neck, and another had a ruptured intestinal organ similar to an appendix.

Eric was the first to arrive at Anaconda. He established his base across the river. He set up the mortar. Although he was under constant surveillance by the orbiting starship, he did not remove his survival suit until he installed a defensive perimeter of motion detectors and cameras. He had better mobility after removing the suit and went to work preparing Anaconda's defense. First he verified that the cameras along the trail at the old observation camp were still working and were well concealed. They would provide good notice on their own. Then he set up the mortar and used the laser rifle to cut a hole through the forest canopy so that there would be a clear field of fire.

With half the day already behind him, Eric nevertheless wanted to be certain that the mortar rounds would drop where he wanted them. He touched a location on the radar-generated map of the mortar's targeting computer, fired a smoke round down toward the trail, and looked to see that the impact point appeared where he expected it to on the targeting computer's map. The targeting system registered the data point, and from that point, the system would be able to target the entire planned battlefield and well beyond the opposite bank of the river.

Next, Eric went down to the village's river crossing, used one of the boats to cross over, and then hiked along the shore upstream to the point across from the planned battlefield. There he prepared a position for the rocket gun. He spent almost two full hours building up a low breastwork with logs cut down with the laser rifle. The position was well camouflaged by small trees and brush yet was not blocked by so much vegetation that the rocket gun's field of fire would be blocked. The battlefield, the area to just beyond the mortar team, and the river crossing would all be in range of this position. It would be able to cover the trail and the river crossing and would anchor the flank on the village side of the river in the event the Vikmoor had crossed the river upstream.

He was not sure what to expect when he went into the village to prepare the final position. After consulting with Reggie by radio, he decided he wanted to build a final dugout in the center of the village. This would be a fallback position for the rocket team and the final defensive position for the village. From there the far side of the river crossing would be in the rocket launcher's range, and it could be used to cover a withdrawal, an attack from across the river, or an attack into the village from any direction. Eric went to the trading post to notify the closest person the village had to someone of authority—the innkeeper—of what he was going to do. The innkeeper did not stop him, but neither would he try to get anyone to help with the construction. The villagers still refused to have anything to do with fighting in any way.

Reggie's team arrived the next day. By this time, Apsel's bowman was unconscious and had to be carried on a stretcher. Rather than put the village into a panic about the infected man, Reggie decided to let the bowman, the woman, Apsel, Apsel's other men, and the released prisoners stay at the base with Judy. Judy could operate the mortar alone, but Apsel and his men could help defend the position in the event Eric's right flank was turned by the Vikmoor. If they did have to retreat, they could be covered by the rocket gun. Reggie would be operating the rocket gun. He could easily cover the trail and if necessary fall back to the dugout inside Anaconda to cover the river crossing. He would still be able to cover the village's flank on the near side of the stream in the event the Vikmoor executed an upstream river crossing. Eric would position himself directly in the Vikmoor's path on the trail. Wearing the survival suit and armed with stun grenades, a stun gun, and a laser rifle, he would constitute a formidable force.

Each element of the defense would be supported by at least one other, and they would have the advantage of an interior line of defense. The front was extended as much as possible so that the flanks could not be turned or the defenders totally bypassed. The plan was to stop the Vikmoor in the narrow confines of the trail along the river. From the position at the observation camp far back on the hill, aided with intelligence provided by the reconnaissance cameras, Judy would be able to supply supporting fire with the mortar over the whole of Eric's position as well as keep the right flank from being turned. Reggie, Paul, and Mark would be at the bunker at the opposite side of the river from Eric with the rocket gun and stun guns. From there, they would be able to use the rocket gun to support Eric and anchor his left flank. Furthermore, both the mortar and the rocket gun were within range of each other's position, and each could provide supporting fire to the other, thereby thwarting any impromptu counterattacks. If the defenses were overwhelmed or turned at any point, everyone was to fall back to the center of the village and from there fight a retreating action all the way to Poplarville, if necessary. If there was a split in the line between Judy and Eric, Judy was authorized to take her people, retreat into the woods, and fall back to the lander. Eric was to fall back to the river crossing where he would receive supporting fire from the rocket gun while he executed his river crossing. If Judy was not cut off, she was to meet him at the crossing with Apsel and the others, and the total force would be reunited at the village's central defensive position.

The Vikmoor attack came in the early morning the day after Reggie's arrival. A full hour's warning was given to the defenders by the *Cutty Sark*. The Vikmoor were walking in a fairly long column, and as they turned the final curve in the trail before reaching Anaconda, they came to Eric, standing alone in his survival suit in the middle of the trail. All of the attackers were soon within range of all three defensive positions, but the only thing the lead Vikmoor elements could see was Eric standing alone just beyond the curve of the trail. The Vikmoor hesitated for only a moment before rushing toward him in a frenzied attack that was a tidal wave of anger and revenge. Eric immediately threw two stun grenades as far forward toward the Vikmoor ranks as he could. This was immediately followed by the distant thump of the mortar being fired, which was soon complemented by an explosion between Eric and the onrushing enemy. At the same time, Reggie let loose with the rocket gun and fired a round of smoke and a stun grenade into the center of the column. All this failed to even slow the Vikmoor surge, as those who fell were replaced by those still coming. Arrows flew. With upheld daggers and battle axes, the attackers raced straight at Eric, some donning their own gas masks and throwing their own mustard gas as they ran. Eric stood erect and unmoving in the center of the trail, directly in their path. Arrows bounced off his survival suit as he emptied his stun gun into the closest attackers. He fired off a stun grenade and an explosive grenade directly at his feet, but still the Vikmoor came on until he was smothered in their advance. Ax blades fell against his arms and shoulders, and a dagger stabbed at his ribs while he fought to keep hold of the laser rifle. He twisted from right side to left, broke free, and fired a seething beam of laser light, cutting two of his attackers in half before being smothered a second time. Then, as the gun was ripped from his hands, he reached down, grabbed an ax from a fallen Vikmoor, and fought hand to hand—burying the ax in one man's chest before lunging toward the Vikmoor who had taken the laser rifle. As the alien struggled to understand the firing mechanism, Eric swung the ax roundabout directly into the left arm at the shoulder. Crying out in pain and fear, the alien dropped the deadly rifle and fell to the ground. Stun grenades, explosive rounds, and the enemy's mustard gas were now exploding all around him as the mortar and rocket teams concentrated their supporting fire and the Vikmoor advanced with their own bombs.

Eric grabbed the fallen rifle. Five more Vikmoor nearly reached him, but he dropped them with the laser. It was only then that he realized that the Vikmoor had used some of their own mustard gas against him, and that although many of them had donned gas masks, many more had not, and a full score had fallen to that gas. Nevertheless, if Eric had not been there to stand in their path, at least twenty Vikmoor would have gotten through—more than enough to terrorize the village. But soon all of the attackers were either in retreat, dead, lying wounded, or asleep from the stun grenades. Eric pulled the ones without masks away from the mustard gas and called Judy down to help with the injured. Nothing that the aliens had done had penetrated Eric's survival suit. The defense had held.

As Eric was administering first aid to the most injured Vikmoor, he realized that almost all of them were developing open sores of the type described by Reggie. He immediately let him know, and Reggie informed Elizabeth.

Reggie, Paul, and the slowly healing Mark crossed the river to investigate and get samples from the sick Vikmoor. They had not made arrangements for handling prisoners. But some of the Vikmoor Eric had gone at with the ax and laser were so badly injured that Reggie decided to have the two rescued men put them on stretchers and take him up to the camp where the astronauts established a field hospital. Several of the Vikmoor had been badly injured by their own mustard gas, and they would need treatment, too. Judy, the alien girl Mahria, and Paul began treating them as best they could. Eric stood guard over the battlefield, and three stun grenades had to be set off to ensure that the remaining Vikmoor attackers remained asleep while the injured were carried to the makeshift hospital.

While they slept, Mark took tissue samples from as many of the Vikmoor as he could, photographed each subject, noted whether the subjects appeared to have the sores, and matched each sample with the visual record and his notes. He did this with ten of the sleeping Vikmoor. By the time he finished, all of the aliens that Reggie intended to take to the hospital had been safely transported. Only then did the defenders retire from the battlefield.

As the remaining Vikmoor awoke, they did not threaten Anaconda but instead stumbled back toward their own village—defeated.

CHAPTER 18

Death

Apsel's ill bowman rested at the hospital. Elizabeth did her best to treat him, but it was clear that he was dying from the sleeping sickness. Likewise, a trail of dead and sick men streamed forth from the scene of the battle and back to the Vikmoor village. Apparently, they too had the disease. As the Vikmoor returned to their village, the scope of their defeat became clear, such that nearly everyone in the village burned inside with their desire for revenge even as the sour black smoke spread forth from the funeral pyres of the plague victims. The extent of their catastrophe was obvious even from the orbiting starship.

More samples were taken from the bowman and flown by robot plane to the lander for analysis, uplink, and remote study aboard the orbiting starship. But even the medicine of the *Cutty*'s scientists could still do little but prolong the agony and fear of the disease, and Apsel's bowman soon joined the Vikmoor in death—the final destination for the short war's victor and vanquished alike.

CHAPTER 19

Recovery

While the astronauts and their allies treated the sick and wounded, Elizabeth continued her research, and Jake continued to try to diagnose the problems with the lander's flight control systems. Three more days passed before Jake discovered what had gone wrong with the repairs. He explained the problem to Reggie by radio.

"The flight computer we cannibalized from the lifeboat was too limited to process the signals from the additional gyroscopes of the lander, which had two more than the lifeboat. Both of the vehicles use a democratic processing system. That is, all of the gyroscopes send data to the computer; it compares their signals, accepts the data of the majority, and shuts down the loser, which is presumed to be faulty.

"It's so simple that it took me awhile to find it," Jake explained. "The lifeboat's computer couldn't process the signals from the additional gyroscopes and send commands to the controls quickly enough to make good attitude adjustments. And you need a computer's help when you're in hover mode in that bird. It's just too unstable. But what happened to us was worse than not having a computer. The computer was working, but the processing was slow. So the system kept reacting to conditions that were actually slightly in the past. When Eric tried to compensate for the ship's roll by giving it more opposite power, that power was added to automated stabilization commands just given, though given late, by the computer. That's why she almost rolled over."

"What's the fix?"

"Easy. I disconnected two of the gyroscopes. We'll lose some redundancy, but we'll be okay."

More good news came just a few days later as the research and experiments concerning the disease were brought to a conclusion. The *Cutty*'s chief scientist discussed the findings of the shipboard scientists and bio technicians with Elizabeth, and she radioed Reggie at the camp and advised him of their progress.

"We've been analyzing the problem with electron microscopes, recombinant DNA studies, nuclear magnetic resonance, X-ray crystallography, and computer modeling. Apparently, these people are all infected by a latent virus—or more correctly a system of two viruses. We don't think it's natural. It isn't present in the bodies in the cemetery from before the war, and it's only remotely related to any other viruses on the planet. Actually, the disease works in two stages. The first stage uses a retrovirus to restructure the host's polygenic chains relating to aggression. It sets up a cross-link to the stress factors chain. It first hits in a region of the brain structurally similar to the human temporal limbic system. Then, when a person becomes aggressive, immunoglobulin levels are reduced such that the second virus—a disease similar to Earth's herpes simplex virus—takes hold. Just as old Earth's herpes could lie dormant but break out when the subject was feeling stress, the same effect was engineered here for victims feeling aggressive."

"I've seen anxiety weaken immune systems," Reggie noted. "You're telling me this disease does the same thing with aggression?"

"Yes, sir. Feelings of aggression in the infected victims drastically reduce their version of their immunoglobulin levels. This is done with the retrovirus that alters the normal DNA of the aggression polygenic chain. It's even tied into the endocrine system. We can tell that the immunoglobulin levels of Apsel's sick bowman were definitely low, and they were also low in that sick Anacondan friend of yours back at Anaconda. They are much higher in the bodies of subjects who died of natural causes. They are also much higher in Apsel and his men who aren't sick. We suspect that that's because Apsel and his men were fighting just to help us, not out of any particular aggression. But from what I've been told, that bowman of his that got sick did get caught up in the heat of battle. That's probably why he got the disease. There are definite differences in the gene structure of those who died before and after the war, so we think this was a disease that was engineered—engineered for military purposes."

"Engineered to attack only those who themselves were in the mood to fight," added Reggie. "Neat. I guess that seemed like a pretty moral weapon, but it wasn't exactly nonlethal. And it looks like it affects those who are merely trying to defend themselves as much it does attackers— because even they get emotional. Is there a fix?"

"We think so. We're developing a cocktail consisting of antiviral metabolites and a vaccine. That way, we can both inhibit the further assembly of viral DNA and get the body's own immune systems up. We'll also try to manufacture a retrovirus of our own and use it to reengineer the biological makeup back to what it was before. The genetic engineering will protect anyone who doesn't have the active disease and spread naturally over generations. And we think we can manufacture a more benign version of the disease itself that will also spread naturally, and although it will produce flulike symptoms, it will provide a natural immunization to the sleeping sickness. Over time, the engineering and the inoculation should spread across the planet. But establishing some nodes should accelerate the process. As for us, we aren't affected. We've confirmed that our biology is so different that the disease is not a threat to us. We should be able to purge it pretty easily. But we're still not sure if this relates to the general deterioration of the planet, other than a decrease in the population."

"Mark, come over here," Reggie called to his exoanthropologist. "I have Elizabeth here." He indicated the communicator.

"Elizabeth, this explains something that I've been thinking ever since we saw that Vikmoor village. I've always noticed that some people are people of action—doers and achievers—while others walk through life half-asleep. Most of the people on this planet are apathetic. I've got a theory that I want to bounce off you and Mark."

Mark sat at the campfire, and Reggie explained what they had learned.

"Mark, what would happen to a society in which all tendencies to aggression were bred out?" he asked.

"Well, I guess it's possible. Domesticated animals are docile because they are bred to be that way. There is a process called 'intra specific selection,' in which interspecies breeding of a certain trait seems to distill that trait. I guess it would be possible to breed a trait into or out of nascent life as well. Even a psychological trait, I suppose."

"But what would that do?"

"Theoretically, aggression is related to defense of the young, selection of leaders by rival fights, mate selection, balanced distribution of animals over the available environment, and it's a driving force of motivation. Take away aggression, and you take away leadership selection, motivation, and defense."

"That's sure consistent with the lack of leadership and motivation and the general deteriorating condition of Anaconda."

"But what about the Vikmoor?" Elizabeth asked.

"I think I understand," continued Mark. "The lion on the hunt doesn't attack out of anger or aggression. Killing is simply what it does to get food. The water buffalo that a lion attacks hasn't done anything to provoke aggression. The counteroffensive of mobbing, as birds mob to defend nests from a predator, is more closely related to aggression. At least the emotions are more intense."

"The Vikmoor village appears to originally have been a penitentiary," interjected Reggie. "People who just went out and took what they wanted because they lacked the moral compulsion to do otherwise. They took and take because they see nothing wrong with it. So their raiding parties have not trigged the disease in themselves, only in those who it angered. However, the lack of coordinated defenses and the absence of real growth indicate that the disease has not left it untouched. Internal struggles for dominance have still taken their toll. You have the same lack of motivation and leadership that you do at Anaconda, except on a lower scale because of the different cultures. The Vikmoor raid and take what they need because they are on the hunt, not because they've been provoked. But when we attacked them, their defensive/aggressive mob instinct took over, and that's when they got sick. I bet if we look, though, we can find a spike in Vikmoor graves from the disease deaths from the time when it first hit. I bet the prisons held plenty of folks who were just plain mad at society—maybe rightfully so. We've discovered few cultures that are truly just and not in some way arbitrary in the distribution of justice, opportunity, and resources. Some inmates may have been truly angry at society, and it was acting out that anger that landed them in prison. Being in prison would not necessarily have terminated their emotions. They would have fallen to the disease."

Paul had joined them and was listening to the discussion. "I see. It really even explains Poplarville. It is an old scientific community. Most of its members are devoted to learning and education. Like absentminded professors, the concept of leadership is foreign to them. Without competition for leadership, the virus was seldom active. So they still have some leadership and motivation, even though the motivation is more closely related to the hunt than aggressive mobbing.

"Of course, some of their scientists have been motivated more by a desire for the power that comes with success—such as more resources and perceived prestige—than they have by altruistic motives of learning. So even Poplarville has had some internal competition and its share of deaths. That's why there's deterioration even in Poplarville. They would have had some scientists and administrators and would-be administrators vying for power. A lot of their leaders have died, so even that society isn't firing on all its jets."

"But they do manage to keep some of the old equipment going," noted Mark.

"Yes, they were sure able to keep that particle beam generator in repair, even though they were clueless as to what it did. That thing almost killed us all," Paul noted.

"I imagine it was originally part of a ballistic missile defense system," Reggie added. "But when the war started, instead of the full-scale missile attack that everyone was expecting, they were hit with high-altitude EMP blasts. That would explain the isolated hotspots we found. Ironically, both sides attacked without being adequately prepared defensively. The EMP blasts put society so far back into the Stone Age that they just couldn't recover. Especially when the antiaggression virus hit. Once the virus was introduced, it must have gotten out of hand and spread over the whole planet, judging by the lack of organized civilization visible from orbit. Maybe it mutated. And the military was affected because even a professional military has brotherhood and defense of homeland cultures that have emotional mobbing-instinct-type consequences tied with downright anger and desires for vengeance."

Apsel heard the discussion and sat down at the fire.

"And," added Elizabeth, "those guys in Poplarville are still managing to crank out mustard gas."

"Evidently," Mark said, "some villages are trying to resist. Maybe they're evolving a defense. It could even be psychological. They could be resisting out of cold-blooded logic, just like a lion hunts out of cold-blooded logic."

"Hence the demand for the mustard gas," agreed Reggie.

Even though Apsel now realized that Reggie was no normal trader, he still stood up for his village. "Don't forget, with those gas bombs we trade for the food and supplies that allow us to continue our studies, our research, and even create new pesticides—and the pesticides help everyone."

"We know that you mean no harm," said Reggie. "Okay, Elizabeth, let's call the *Cutty* and work on a fix. I'm not abandoning these people."

CHAPTER 20

Freedom

With the disease now understood, the starship's researchers quickly developed a cure for the fatal "sleeping sickness." Connors decided it was time to send down a team of scientists and technicians with a batch of the drug and the necessary equipment to manufacture more. They all received alien disguises so that they could work directly with the local populace while a damage-control party helped speed repair of the lander's hull breach.

Lander 2 had its protective screens, normally employed only at interplanetary speeds, at full power as it drilled through the alien atmosphere. But Reggie's sabotage work had not been in vain, and the landing was unopposed. The vehicle set down on the beach next to the damaged *Lander 1.* It took little time for the damage-control party to disembark themselves and their equipment and for the cargo handlers to unload the sky truck from the hold. From there the sky truck would be flown to Reggie's camp, where he had cleared a landing zone with the laser rifle. Reggie wanted to take the sky truck to Poplarville and knew he needed to have Apsel with him if he wanted to have a friendly reception. So while he waited for the sky truck's arrival, he explained to Apsel that he had not told him the whole truth about the village "beyond the long lake." But Apsel was still not told the whole story.

"Like your people," Reggie explained, "we have some knowledge that is dangerous. So, like your people, we know that we must keep our knowledge to ourselves. So do not be alarmed by what you are about to see."

Apsel stood with Reggie at the edge of the landing zone. Soon the low rumble of the sky truck's dual engines echoed through the forest—first faintly in the distance and then loudly overhead as the sky truck appeared above them and threw the deafening blast of its downwash into the clearing.

Apsel stood unafraid but did unconsciously take one step back as the craft descended and settled on its landing struts. The sky truck's crew quickly unloaded enough medicine to treat all of Anaconda. Judy and Elizabeth would take care of that. Then Reggie and Apsel climbed aboard, and in the short time it took Reggie to introduce Apsel to the seven scientists and technicians, the vehicle had completed a hop to a small clearing just out of Poplarville's view. Apsel now understood clearly that his new friends were from a very different place. He did not have the imagination to guess that they were from another planet, but in all other ways, they did seem alien to him. After landing, neither Apsel nor Reggie said much during the short hike from the sky truck to Poplarville. Apsel again got Reggie past the guards. This time, however, Apsel led him straight to the director without being summoned.

Reggie explained to the director about the sleeping sickness and his own people's willingness to help cure it. The astronaut was then given an audience with the research review committee. It was, at first, a difficult meeting, because some of the sabotage of the subterranean equipment had been discovered, and the scientists had surmised that Apsel's two strange friends were somehow responsible. But with Blaed dead from the sleeping sickness, no one was concerned about the loss of a machine that provided no practical or educational benefits. Being men of logic, these Poplarville scientists put their apprehensions aside when they were confronted with Reggie's explanation of the disease and a course of action for its remedy. They readily accepted the drug.

The biggest obstacle came in explaining the altruistic notion of helping others without expecting to immediately get something back in trade. Galtonians understood nonaggression, but passivity did not automatically translate into either charity or a willingness to act on the utilitarian benefits of a global social contract based at that time on nothing more than a common humanity. Once the villagers agreed to help, the *Cutty*'s scientists and technicians were brought in to lay out the plans for the mass production and distribution of the antiviral metabolites and vaccines needed to fight the sleeping sickness on a planetary scale.

Galton would soon be free of the abnormalities imposed by the artificial antiaggression disease—the sleeping sickness. Soon, the planet's biological and cultural evolution would be returned to its natural development.

CHAPTER 21

The Great War

Apsel and his two men stayed with Reggie. Upon returning to the observation camp, Reggie had suggested that Apsel and his men escort Mahria back to Anaconda to help Judy and Elizabeth administer the medicine there.

It was not a happy homecoming for the girl. Upon returning to her cabin, she found it deserted and soon learned of her husband's death. His mother described his death from the sleeping sickness. "It was his anger for the Vikmoor," she said. "It burned in his heart when they took you. He wanted to fight them to get you back. He tried not to have such thoughts, but they got the best of him. He brooded for days. Please think of him as you knew him, a man of peace, a good man."

Nearly all capacity for anger had been bred out of Mahria, but at this comment, she snapped. It was the combination of the unreleased pressures from her ordeal, the frustration of helplessness, and the loss of the young husband she barely had had time to love. To hear his own mother talk as if he had done something wrong by wanting to fight to help her escape was more than she could bear.

Manifested as tears, her anger came pouring out. "He *should* have helped me," she sobbed. "These men came."

She pointed at Apsel. "They saved me. They brought me home. I, too, was good, but the Vikmoor took me. I did not fight, and your son did not fight. Why should he die?" Her tears stopped, replaced by determination. "It is not fair."

Her face was contorted in anger. "The gods do not kill us; men kill us. I have learned that this disease is not from the gods but from men." She looked up at Apsel, who was standing at her side. He nodded. Mahria was calming down now. She relaxed.

"I am sorry, Mother Denia," Mahria said softly. "But we have learned that sometimes it is right to fight."

"Sometimes there is a need," Apsel added. "Perhaps I show love and faith by not fighting someone who has wronged me, but it is up to the rest of us to help someone who is being hurt, and we must fight evil."

"We learned that from the visitors," Mahria explained. "And they gave us something to keep us from getting the sickness. We have some for the rest of you."

"We will put an end to the Vikmoor taking from you," Apsel said firmly. He had decided he liked the girl and wanted to stay. Besides, he had learned much from the visitors. It seemed like helping was the right thing to do.

Mahria explained to the villagers the origins of the disease and administered the medicine to those who would take it. Together, she and Apsel organized some of the villagers to begin the reconstruction and completion of the wooden blockade that encircled part of the village. It was difficult at first to convert the villagers to the new philosophy. But having lost their priest, they had no other leader, and so eventually they began to follow her. Then, thinking and reasoning through what to do next, Mahria chose some of the village's strongest, young converted men and women and began training them for war. Apsel taught those who were willing but not good soldiers how to make bows, arrows, and spears. He taught the less-proficient students how to assemble the less-skill-demanding fire arrows and firebombs. He taught the new soldiers how to use their weapons and chose leaders to continue the training. The Vikmoor had been right about Anaconda having hidden food. Mahria used the promise of a safe refuge and food for the winter to convince Gruff, Bodolf, and other traders to move their families to Anaconda. She believed that the traders had the kind of attitude Anaconda needed if it were to fight and survive.

Mahria and Apsel stood in relative rest at the beginning of what was to be a particularly intense day of training. The sun was just rising, and from low on the horizon, it sent its rays to paint the single band of clouds in the eastern sky a soft red. It was the beginning of a new day.

"We are ready to attack the Vikmoor," she began. "The disease will no longer stop us. We may do as we will, and we will put an end to all of their stealing from us once and for all, and we will take back what they have taken from us."

Apsel looked at her and wondered if this was the lesson the visitors had really meant to be learned. He knew that the loss of life inflicted on the Vikmoor in Mark's rescue had taken a terrible toll. They had already been short of food, and now those remaining were underfed, weak, and diseased. Many more would die through the winter. They had never been treated as they should have been. Yet Anaconda was not his village and so not his place to argue. And he did not want Mahria to think him weak if he resisted fighting. But he knew that he must. He knew that he must set them in a new direction. *Because,* he reasoned silently to himself, *if the Vikmoor take food because, as Mark told me they said, it is the only way they know how to get food, will they not still need food even if we defeat them in a great war? What about showing our love by helping those who are hungry and sick? Should we not stand beside one another in hard times? If I show no love for them but only anger or indifference, have I not lost who I am and am supposed to be?* He was not sure what to do next, but he knew that if he went to Vikmoor, he would have to do something other than go as an enemy.

CHAPTER 22

Homeward Bound

Future contact teams would have complete surveys with which to plan return missions to this planet now named Galton III—if there were to be any return missions to this unremarkable planet. But for this crew, it was time to go home.

With the entire crew complement safely aboard, *Cutty Sark*'s energy generators again were brought to maximum power. With mass dampers engaged, the USS *Cutty Sark* arrowed toward Earth. The principles of action and reaction being better understood as applied to stellar navigation than social endeavors, that course was more certain and exact than that set for the Galtonians.

Printed in the United States
By Bookmasters